She had to say goodbye

"Aram, I want to thank you," Zelda said quickly. "It was kind of you to see me all this way but I don't want to waste any more of your time."

"I've got plenty of time to waste—you're the one with the plane to catch," he said slowly. "What's the matter, Zelda? Running away?" He spoke in that deep voice she found as exciting as the nearness of his body.

She tried to look as though she didn't know what he was talking about. "Running away? Of course I'm not. What would I be running away from?" Then she turned abruptly to do just that.

Too late. His hand was on her arm, turning her gently around to face him.

"Me?" he suggested, and held her eyes with his own.

Lucy Keane first started writing when she was six. After earning a degree in English at Oxford, she subsequently pursued a colourful career that ranged from working in the wheeling and dealing world of finance to teaching nursery rhymes to four-year-olds in New Delhi. Her innumerable hobbies include drinking hot chocolate in the ski huts of the French Alps and digging up Roman drains on archaeological sites. Lucy is an obsessional traveler, and a dedicated researcher into real-life romance.

Books by Lucy Keane

HARLEQUIN ROMANCE
3136—FALSE IMPRESSIONS

MAGIC CARPETS
Lucy Keane

Harlequin Books

TORONTO • NEW YORK • LONDON
AMSTERDAM • PARIS • SYDNEY • HAMBURG
STOCKHOLM • ATHENS • TOKYO • MILAN

Original hardcover edition published in 1991
by Mills & Boon Limited

ISBN 0-373-03178-5

Harlequin Romance first edition February 1992

MAGIC CARPETS

CHAPTER ONE

THE dealer, an elderly bearded villager in a long white robe and headcloth, shook his head thoughtfully. His English was more than good enough for the purposes of their transactions, but it was his gestures and facial expressions that Zelda followed most closely. Now, he stroked the carpet with one brown, lean-fingered hand as he spoke—just possessiveness, she wondered, or a sign that he was considering her offer?

'No, no, no, no.' His shrewd dark eyes weighed her up. 'You will ruin me!' He had a fatherly, indulgent tone, but how much could she trust in it?

Experience had taught her that it wasn't to her advantage to betray too much knowledge about what she was buying, or to seem too eager for the rug she really wanted. Her offhand interest had been well simulated up to now, and it wouldn't do to spoil her chances. She shrugged, and glanced round the small dark room where rolls of carpets of varied sizes were stacked against the walls, all probably destined for a smarter, and therefore more expensive dealer's in Aleppo.

Then, from a pair of wide grey eyes, she gave the old Arab a look that few men could resist—even her disciplinarian of a father, as she had known from a disgracefully early age.

'It's too much money,' she said, her deep, slightly husky voice sounding a note of regret. 'Haven't you got anything else like this? The same sort of colours?'

He shook his head again. 'No, no. This is the only one. This is a very good carpet—very special.'

It was special all right. It was Turkish, of very fine quality indeed, and not the sort of thing she had expected to find out in an obscure Syrian village.

'Can't I see some more? What about the one over there?' She pointed a slim finger in the direction of a half-unrolled rug. If she could find anything else she could appear more interested in, and that was worth buying, she could perhaps get him to consider a sort of package deal. That way she might be able to get a substantial reduction on the one she really wanted, without him suspecting that it was the Turkish rug she was after and putting up the price accordingly. He probably knew it was good—but not that good. She could make four or five times what she hoped to pay for it when she sold it again in London.

'This?' He indicated the one she had selected, and flicked his fingers at the lithe, quick-eyed boy who was watching all their negotiations from the carpet-stacked shadows. 'Hassan!'

The boy jumped to his feet, and unrolled the rug, giving it a quick professional flip so that it unfurled in a bright kaleidoscope before Zelda, where she sat cross-legged on one of the offerings she had rejected earlier.

She took a sip from her cup of dark, aromatic coffee, and gave the dealer an enthusiastic glance. Although she didn't have as much interest in it for its own sake, the carpet would do very well if she could negotiate buying it with the other. She and her partners would sell it at a profit; they had a couple of others of similar origin in their warehouse already.

She would have to be careful. The present cash-flow situation was pretty dire, and money was still a big problem for them. If she couldn't come back with some real bargains, there might not be a Magic Carpets Company for much longer.

'For Pete's sake don't spend too much,' Melanie had warned anxiously, just before Zelda had left London a couple of months earlier. 'We've got to make mega-profits on everything we sell if we're going to afford to eat for the next six months! The overheads on the warehouse are about the last straw just now.'

'Who's got the best eye for a bargain in the business, then?' Zelda had retorted cheekily. 'You mind how you talk to your chief carpet buyer! Rick couldn't tell a genuine Baluchistan from a cheap Brussels off-cut, and neither could you if I hadn't already put a label on it!'

And, when it came to striking those all-important bargains, Zelda knew her appearance was in her favour. Far from looking like an experienced professional, she deliberately played up the youthful traveller image with her baggy striped trousers and loose-fitting T-shirt. Even her jewellery was calculated to contribute to the general impression of a girl who liked to collect souvenirs of her wanderings—half a dozen turquoise and silver rings, and an armful of similar bangles and dangling earrings, none of them of any real value.

She also knew she could make use of certain natural assets: a clear-skinned face, with a slightly squared, dimpled chin and wide, appealing grey eyes under a short Twenties-style mop of dark hair, cut in a deep fringe across her forehead. Looking like a boyish teenager might have its drawbacks at parties in London, particularly if she wanted to make an impression on some desirable male who preferred his women blonde and voluptuously curvaceous, but it certainly had its advantages when it came to bargaining in a Middle Eastern bazaar.

No carpet salesman she had yet encountered had suspected for a moment that the eager teenager before him— seemingly on the verge of tears when she couldn't pay the price that would have left him a handsome profit margin—was in fact a twenty-three-year-old dealer in her own right. Most of the company's income to date was due to Zelda's genius in negotiating with a deviousness that would have amazed the wily salesmen if they had been able to see the mind at work behind that ingenuous grey-eyed gaze.

The Syrian looked at her, and she looked at the Syrian.

'You like this one?' he asked, his tone of voice betraying nothing.

'Oh, yes!' she enthused. She fingered it, outwardly admiring, while in reality checking it for flaws, her keen eye noting the dyes, and the evenness of the weave. Casually, almost as though by accident, she flipped a corner and glanced at the back, roughly assessing the number of knots to the square inch and again the expertise with which this particular rug had been woven. It wasn't a bad buy by any standards, but it was still the other she really wanted. That was exceptional, and even at the price he was asking was a once-in-a-lifetime bargain.

She felt no misgivings about getting the better of the Syrian over the deal—if she didn't buy that beautiful rug to make a profit out of it, then someone else would. And her whole livelihood depended on her skill in driving a hard bargain: she couldn't afford to give anything away with the present state of the company.

She began on her favourite tactics.

'You see, friends back home asked me to buy a carpet for them,' she lied. 'I think they would really like this, but they didn't want me to spend too much money.' Then she put down her coffee-cup carefully. 'How much?'

He mentioned a sum, and she let her face fall dramatically.

'I'm not sure I can afford as much as that...' She mentioned another figure, way below his, and laughed when he protested again that she'd ruin him. 'I don't know anything about buying carpets,' she assured him, wide-eyed, 'but your price seems to be awfully high, and I'd like to tell my friend I got a bargain for her.'

She thought the glance he gave her at that point had more than a hint of suspicion about it, and told herself not to overdo the naïve act. She had, after all, picked out the best carpet he had to offer—they mightn't believe in anything like beginner's luck in Syria.

It was at that moment, glancing towards the doorway, that she realised she had an audience. Only a few yards away from the open courtyard of this ramshackle assortment of buildings, which included the dealer's 'shop', stood a tall man. Despite his dark hair and hawk-like features, there was something about him that suggested he wasn't a local.

She hadn't expected to find anyone but Syrians in this tiny village, well off the beaten track. She wasn't even sure where she was—some miles east of Aleppo was about as close as she could get to fixing a map reference. She had accepted a lift into the desert with an elderly Arab villager, a friend of the manager of the small hotel in which she had been staying in Aleppo. The road they had taken had seemed mostly a matter of guesswork, following the marker stones that pointed a way through the endless planes of dusty brown that stretched as far as the eye could see. It was miles from the usual tourist route.

Like many of the more westernised Syrians, her observer was casually dressed in light-coloured jeans and loose-fitting jacket, but it was neither his height nor his clothing that drew her attention immediately among the smaller-statured, more traditionally dressed Arabs—it was the fact that he was wearing an eye-patch.

He looked quite young, in his early thirties perhaps, and it gave him the most extraordinarily rakish air. Fascinated, she stared at him for a moment, and through his good eye, the right one—a curious blue-green like old bottle glass—he stared back at her. He didn't smile, or greet her, or give any of the normal tourist signs of recognition, and after a moment she ignored him, turning back to the dealer.

'Let me see the other carpets again,' she asked, playing the indecisive foreigner. Inwardly, she admired the saintlike patience of the old Arab—even though she knew that bargaining was the breath of life to someone like him and he would be prepared to spend hours over agreeing a price. But she knew what it was to be on the selling end of a deal, and it was only with the greatest difficulty that she could keep her temper with some of the more indecisive customers she'd had to cope with occasionally in London, when they hadn't the first idea of the merits of any of the wares they were purchasing. Because each carpet she had haggled for was something special to her, and she felt that it ought to be properly appreciated, she hated having to part with any of her bargains.

And that was the basic trouble with her, she reflected irrelevantly—a perfectly good head when it came to the mechanics of life, and a treacherous heart. Her mind could sum up a situation perfectly, and then her emotions would come along and spoil all her calculations by making her do just the opposite to what she had decided...

But now she had to concentrate on the next stage of her stratagem. The Syrian hadn't batted an eyelid at her request, and, unfailingly courteous, he summoned Hassan. The boy once again flicked out the half-dozen rugs she had already inspected.

She tried to keep her eyes from betraying her, glancing at the one she really wanted no more than at all the rest. Then she said weakly, 'Oh, I don't know... This...' She fingered the one next to her favourite. 'Or this...' She stroked the fine pile, her eyes guarded. It truly was an exceptional carpet: old, with a silky sheen, the colours subtly contrasting and blending in an ageless design. It would be hard to part with it, if she was successful in buying it.

'Suppose I got two?' This was the vital part of her plan. 'One for my friends and one for me, and they could choose which they liked. I've only got a limited amount of money but——'

'Can I help?' A deep, slightly rough-edged voice cut across her carefully orchestrated opening.

Sitting as she was on the floor, she glanced up what seemed like miles of leg to find the man with the eye-patch towering above her.

'You don't appear to have had much practice at this,' he said blandly. The casual tone belied his keen glance, and she was aware of that one blue-green eye openly assessing her.

'It's quite all right, thank you.' Her smile was disarmingly sweet, despite the gathering storm clouds behind her eyes. If this stranger cut in now, he would wreck an hour's worth of careful preparation!

'No trouble,' he assured her, rather curtly.

She assessed him quickly, in her turn. Funny how one eye looked so much more calculating than two! It was positively unnerving. She wondered what the patch was hiding. It could look quite sinister, given different circumstances. His English was perfect: he surely couldn't be an Arab, despite the aquiline profile and dark looks— his hair was almost blue-black.

Then he said, almost as an afterthought, 'I've had a bit of experience at this sort of thing.'

She could hardly say, 'So have I.' It would have spoilt everything she'd been trying to achieve. 'It really is quite all right.'

'How much did you think you might offer for the two of them?' he asked.

For one unguarded moment, Zelda's tongue ran ahead of her wits. 'That's none of your business!'

His manner, as well as his intereference, annoyed her. He really was too patronising by half! Then she remembered she was supposed to be inexperienced at this sort of thing—naïve, and, presumably, grateful. 'Er—I mean...thank you very much, but I'm sure I can manage.' She hoped it didn't sound too insincere.

Ignoring her attempt at a brush-off, he squatted down to examine the merchandise, running a thumb over the pile, flipping each rug over to scrutinise the back.

Zelda was in agonies.

Stupid dolt! He'd mess it all up!

With an effort, she kept the smile on her pixie face, and silently prayed that the Syrian wouldn't be encouraged to revalue the object of all her strategy as a result of the stranger's interest. He had now spread out the Turkish rug for examination.

Fortunately—he couldn't know anything about carpets, she told herself with relief—the interfering tourist paid no particular attention to it, casting it aside for another not half its quality.

'Why don't you have this one?' he demanded, scrutinising her again in that unnerving way. 'It's got most of the same colours. It might be cheaper, and it'd look just as good on the floor.'

As if she were asking him for his opinion!

'How much?' He turned to the Syrian. A figure was mentioned. 'I'll give you half that.'

Zelda turned to him in open annoyance. 'Look, whose money is it you're bargaining with—mine or yours? I don't want this carpet. If you want it, wait your turn! This gentleman and I were about to come to an agreement.' 'About to' was a wild exaggeration in the context of the lengthy Eastern bargaining sessions she was used to, but Eye-Patch mightn't know that.

He shot her a quick look. They were on a level now—he was still squatting beside her to examine the carpets. For one disconcerting second their eyes held, and in that second she was conscious of more than just his glance. He was very close to her—so close they were almost touching. Her eyes flicked away from his, and she became aware that she had only to stretch out her fingers for them to come into contact with that tanned, strongly muscled arm with its dusting of dark hair, resting casually on his angled knee.

She wasn't sure what she had been able to read in that one good eye—a question? A challenge?—but for a brief moment all thoughts of the carpet went out of her head. A sudden surge of adrenalin through her system made her skin prickle. It must be the unexpectedness of this confrontation with a stranger just when she thought she'd got everything going nicely, she told herself. Antagonism sparked in her own eyes, but there was something about this man that cautioned her that he wasn't to be easily dismissed.

He looked back to the rejected rug, fingering it, seeming quite unruffled by her hostile reception of his intervention.

'Oh?' The hint of scepticism in his tone instantly suggested he was better acquainted with the ways of the East than she would have liked. 'In my experience agreements aren't so easily reached.'

She was on the verge of telling him that if it came to experience she could probably beat him hands down, but something in the way he was watching her warned her to hold her tongue if she wasn't going to let him spoil her dumb tourist act.

'Which rug do you like, then?' he prompted, just as though she were every bit as stupid as she pretended. 'What about this...?'

He was indicating the object of all her carefully laid plans and that unaccountable, almost defensive hostility turned instantly to exasperation. Blast him! He was absolutely ruining her chances. How was she going to play it now?

Quelling her rising irritation, she gave a good imitation of a casual shrug and avoided meeting his gaze. 'I'm not sure. I really want one for my friends...maybe this one for myself...I like the colours. I'm not sure.'

'So what about this?' He was taking over, the Syrian merely looking on passively and Hassan squatting in a corner, glancing from time to time at his father.

The stranger's tone was now casually friendly and he was almost smiling at her, but there was that hidden dimension that still unnerved her, and the calculating eye was continually watching her. Cold as a green glass marble! she told herself crossly.

'Get this one for your friends, and the other one for yourself,' he suggested. 'Perhaps we could arrange a special deal if you were to buy two instead of one?' He cocked an eye—the unpatched one—at the Syrian.

She could have screamed—just what she'd been intending to do all along, of course, but with the wrong carpets!

She began firmly, 'This is very kind of you, Mr...' and hesitated for him to fill in a name in which she had no interest. She wanted to get rid of him as quickly as possible.

'Aram——'

'Mr Aram, but I really don't think——'

'I told you before, it's no trouble.' He hadn't even let her finish the sentence! Then he gave her an unexpected smile that would have dazzled any toothpaste advertiser, though she refused to let it impress her one little bit as she was so thoroughly annoyed by his tiresome persistence. 'I do know a little about bargaining.'

I'll bet you do! she told herself silently. He mightn't know a lot about carpets, but he looked like the sort of man who would negotiate in the white slave trade, buying girls for some rich Arab sheikh—or, no, more probably for himself! There was a kind of latent animal quality in him that was distinctly predatory.

From that point onwards the curious struggle between herself and the stranger intensified, and she found herself doing battle on two fronts at the same time, though the vital negotiations with the Syrian were beginning to take second place. The stranger, while professing to help her, always seemed to be pushing her towards the edge of betraying herself, and once or twice she was overwhelmingly tempted to give up her naïve tourist role just to let him know where he got off. Then she was forced to take a deep breath, and remind herself that it was merely unlucky chance that she had encountered someone whose well-meant intervention should have such a disastrous effect on her. He surely couldn't be doing it deliberately...

'Perhaps this gentleman would like to buy the rug for himself?' she suggested finally, in a tone of mild sarcasm that only just veiled her thorough exasperation. It was a last-ditch attempt to bring the Syrian back into the negotiations, and to hint to her unwanted assistant that it was time he took a rest.

But instantly there was a flash from that blue-green eye.

'Well, if you're no longer interested...' And the immediate result was a bid on his own behalf that just topped her last offer.

It took a while for the full implications to register. For one moment she was actually speechless—what on *earth* did he think he was playing at, cutting in like that? Or did he know more about carpets than he appeared to?

Aware of his scrutiny, Zelda thought furiously. If she entered into open competition with him two things would surely happen: first, if she won, she would end up paying much more than she intended for the rug, and second, she would inevitably betray herself as far too experienced at bargaining for her youthful traveller image, and lose her advantage.

'I thought you were trying to help, but you're making it all so difficult!' she complained, trying to sound tearful in an attempt to appeal to his chivalry—if he had any. It wasn't wholly convincing—too young she'd lost the knack of bursting into tears to get what she wanted, on the discovery that it was only likely to make elder brothers even more resentful. In most circumstances, she was more likely to lose her temper than to cry, but now she regretted the lack of such a feminine accomplishment. It might have achieved more than swearing at him.

Then, on the spur of the moment, a new strategy occurred to her, and she gave in to a dangerous impulse—to bid against him, run him up to a high figure, and then back out! It meant losing the rug, but too bad; she would no longer get it at the price she wanted anyway. And, she discovered quite suddenly and with some surprise— it wasn't like her to get side-tracked from a bargain— that more than anything else now she wanted to get the better of him.

She was well aware of the perils of such a plan—he could play the same trick on her and she couldn't afford the outcome—but there was beginning to be something unexpectedly exhilarating about pitting her wits against him. Despite the fact that they were total strangers, it seemed to her now as though there were a curious bond between them. They shared a liking for the same game: testing each other, trying to read each other's minds, looking for a sign of weakening, the moment when the competitor would back down... She calculated the market price of the rug. She would push him as close as she dared to it, so that with such a marginal profit he might just as well have bought the carpet at home. That would teach him to muscle in on other people's deals!

The Syrian looked on in some amazement as the two foreigners began to bid against each other. They were talking very attractive money, but as the price soared he realised that there was something going on that didn't have very much to do with his carpet.

Then, catching the stranger's eye as they were getting close to what she had estimated as the lowest likely retail price in the English market, way above what the Syrian could hope to ask, Zelda suddenly knew it was time to stop. She didn't know what it was—his appearance, his disconcerting gaze gave nothing away—but an instinct that rarely failed her warned that he was about to back out.

'It's yours,' she said quickly. 'I can't possibly afford to pay all that money for one rug. I wanted to get two— as presents.' There was no harm in keeping up the pretence.

His look of surprise was gratifying, and told her he'd thought she would be unable to resist the temptation to go higher.

'Why did you go up to such a figure, then?' he asked coolly.

'Why did you pretend to be helping me when you wanted it yourself?' she countered. Whew! She'd got out just in time!

'I had the impression you weren't really interested in it after a while.' He sounded coldly dismissive, and instantly she reacted.

'Of course I was interested! I wouldn't have bid against you if I hadn't been!' But she was sure he didn't believe it was as simple as that—he'd guessed what she had been trying to do.

Then, unexpectedly, he grinned at her, that white toothpaste ad grin that she might have thought attractive if she hadn't found him so exasperating. And, just as though it really had been some kind of crazy game, he said, 'OK. Why not start again? Regard that as an interesting exercise and go back to square one?' He turned to the Syrian, and said something to him in Arabic. That annoyed her again, because the Syrian laughed and she suspected that the infuriating 'Mr Aram' was taking advantage of her ignorance of the language to establish a private understanding.

'What did you just say?' she demanded.

'I was trying to explain that that last bit of bargaining was a ... sort of joke between us. Now we'll go back to the serious business of buying the rug for you.'

Zelda glared at him. It didn't seem much like a joke that he had just tried to ruin her deal. But maybe there was a new chance of getting her carpet, although she'd still have to go higher than she had originally intended. Just as well she hadn't quite given herself away.

Eventually, because she was determined that if this man insisted on interfering she was going to end up with the right carpets, she got what she wanted. She couldn't really complain about the price, but she was certain it was higher than she would have negotiated left to her own devices. If she got the chance, out of earshot of the Syrian, she was going to let this tiresome stranger know it.

The deal was concluded with more cups of coffee, and some sticky nutty sweets rather like Turkish delight. Once the business was over, Zelda experienced a curious sense of having been through some ordeal—it was almost the way she had used to feel when she'd come out of some particularly tricky school exam. The old Arab didn't seem too dissatisfied with the outcome of the extraordinary negotiations, and she was sure now that he really hadn't known what he'd got in that carpet. He told her that he had acquired it from a tourist, who had been travelling down from Turkey with several other rugs he had bought there, and then had decided to exchange one of them for a selection of the local village-made ones that the Syrian had to offer.

Stupid tourist! she commented to herself. And lucky me—even if I have paid more than I wanted thanks to that interfering idiot Mr Aram.

Then it struck her, belatedly, that 'idiot' was hardly the right word to describe her mysterious companion. That calculating look in his eye was far too keen.

Zelda had resigned herself to a long wait until her Arab acquaintance with the truck should pass through. She planned to fill in the time before her lift with exploring what there was of the village and reading a book she had brought with her. But, during the polite exchanges over coffee, it became obvious that her unwanted bargaining assistant had other ideas for her.

'What time did you say your Arab friend would be coming back?' he asked, raising a dark eyebrow over the unpatched eye.

'Not before seven,' she admitted with some reluctance. It had occurred to her that he might have his own vehicle, and that he might offer her a lift, but she was

in two minds about accepting. On the one hand, it would
be very convenient to get back early. She was hoping to
set out for the Turkish border the next day, and needed
time to sort out her packing. But on the other hand she
didn't want to see more of this predatory-looking individual than was absolutely necessary. He had already
intruded in a very unwelcome way into her life, and she
didn't want to encourage his interest in her even though
she was half prepared to admit to herself—now that her
frustration with him had died down a bit—that he was,
in a dangerous kind of way, undeniably attractive.

'Why not come along with me? I hired a car in Aleppo.
There's another village I'd like to have a look at not far
from here, but I'll be back in town long before your
Arab turns up again.'

She shot him a suspicious glance, which wasn't lost
on him, and he gave her a grin she didn't like.

'What's the matter—cold feet about accepting lifts
from strangers? Haven't you already taken a big enough
risk in coming out here with one? I'm an Englishman
and a gentleman. That ought to reassure you.'

You don't look like either! she was about to retort,
but thought better of it. Then she caught a look in his
eye that was unmistakably amusement, and her irritation was suddenly mingled with something like relief.

Although she might act the naïve twit when it suited
her purposes, Zelda was a seasoned traveller. Experience
had taught her that she could usually rely on gut instinct
when it came to judging people in circumstances of this
sort. The aquiline features and rakish eye-patch might
make this man look like some desert raider, and there
was a powerful aura of masculinity about him that she
had been uncomfortably aware of from the start, but,
despite the fact she didn't like him, and resented his interference—even if it was well meant—she didn't think
he offered any serious threat to her.

'What's the interest in visiting another village?' she queried. 'And how come you ended up in this one? It's a bit off the beaten track, isn't it?'

'I might ask the same questions of you,' he replied. 'I'm just the average innocent tourist in search of local handiwork, but I'm not so sure about you. Average you are *not*—and innocent I very much doubt!'

'Speak for yourself. There wasn't much innocence about the way you were trying to do me out of my rug just now!' He gave an amused glance, and, despite her annoyance with him, she decided she rather liked the way one lock of hair flipped over his forehead. His hair wasn't straight; there was a slight wave to it ... Then she realised she was staring at him, and he had noticed.

'Well, am I giving you a lift or not?' he asked with heavy patience. 'I'd like to get going in the next few minutes.'

'I suppose I might as well,' she said rather ungraciously. 'It's an awfully long wait until Farouq gets back.' He gave her another penetrating look from that single disconcerting eye. 'Suit yourself,' he said abruptly, and turned to the Arab to begin the process of leave-taking.

Zelda and the dealer parted amicably, shaking hands on the bargain while the dutiful Hassan packed her newly purchased rugs into the boot of the battered car her companion had hired.

'How come you're travelling around like this on your own?' he asked, once they were headed out, at what seemed to her to be very literally breakneck speed, into the desert. The car bounced and ricocheted from one pot-hole to another, and had no seatbelts.

Zelda was still simmering from the results of his earlier high-handed interference in her carefully laid stratagems. She was sorely tempted to give a crushing reply, revealing herself to be the experienced dealer she was, but decided against it—she might be able to use the information later to better advantage.

'As you said—I'm a tourist. I took a trip down to Damascus, but I decided to break away and see things for myself. This is my last day here and I wanted to get out into the desert. The manager of the hotel I'm staying at got me this lift—he was the person who told me about that carpet dealer.' At least some of it was true. 'Do you have to drive so fast?'

She didn't know whether to clutch the seat or the top of her head—twice it felt as though her skull was about to go through the roof.

'There's no third gear,' he said, with a total lack of concern. 'It's either this or crawl along in second.'

'Why on earth did you hire such a clapped-out old crate in the first place?' she demanded scornfully. 'Anyone could tell by looking at it that it's no good!'

'You don't mince your words, do you?' She was aware of his glance. His good eye, the right one, was on her side. 'It was the only one they had at the time. It makes a change.'

'From what?'

'From what I normally drive. But you haven't exactly answered my question—what *are* you doing on your own?' She turned sideways to look at him, studying the clearly etched profile—the hooked nose and strong jawline reminding her of some Roman emperor off an old coin. His large hands were strong and competent on the wheel, and there was a determined look to the well-shaped mouth that suggested a man who had complete confidence in his own ability. Whoever he was, this 'Mr Aram', he wasn't a nobody—there was something about him that would set him apart from the crowd wherever he found himself.

Maybe she would take him down a peg or two. He might think he was accustomed to bargaining, but he really didn't know much about the value of carpets, judging from the way he had conducted the negotiations earlier.

'I've got a bone to pick with you,' she said, with careful emphasis. 'Just why did you think you had to interfere with my haggling session back there?'

He glanced at her quickly. 'You didn't seem too sure of what you were doing...' Had she really taken him in? On reflection, that earlier comment about innocence had been very two-edged—it could have been more than just the sexual innuendo it had seemed at first. 'I don't think you paid an unfair price for what you got in the end—do you?'

'No. Not unfair,' she agreed reluctantly. 'But it cost me more than I was prepared to pay. I could have got both of those rugs cheaper if you hadn't butted in.'

'Oh, I don't think you could,' he commented with an irritating coolness. 'It looked to me as though that old Arab was going to run you up to quite a high figure if you weren't careful. But I'm sorry if you think I wasn't any help to you. You're almost making me feel guilty.' He didn't sound regretful—or guilty—in the least.

She shot him a quick look. *'Almost?'*

'It was up to you to finalise the deal, and, if you hadn't wanted it, you could have backed out. Judging by the trick you tried to play on me just now, you don't strike me as the kind of person who would just sit back and let it all happen if you didn't agree to it. But if you're in money difficulties I'll buy one of them from you.'

'I don't want to sell.'

He ignored her. 'You could make an instant profit on it. Tell you what—you keep the pretty one and I'll buy the other—the odd one. In fact, I'll offer you half as much again as you paid for it.'

'You mean the Tur—the one the dealer got from the tourist?' she corrected hastily. 'Why?'

He glanced across at her, and the car gave another lurch. 'I've just told you—I liked it. And I feel kind of guilty that you think you could have got a better bargain on your own. I don't agree with you, but there's no way we're going to prove it and you're entitled to your opinion.'

'It so happens I like that carpet too. What about buying the other one instead?'

'It wouldn't go with my colour schemes.'

'So you want it for home?'

He nodded, and there was a pause. Why did she get the feeling she was continually being pushed into something against her will? She had only to say no—there was nothing difficult about that. It must be because he was such a forceful character, interfering with her negotiations with the Syrian despite her, and now trying to persuade her into a further deal she didn't want. She hadn't even been one hundred per cent sure about accepting the lift from him, and here she was, sitting beside him out in the middle of nowhere. Still, she might as well try to ensure that it all worked to her advantage.

She suggested, 'What about three and a half times what I paid for it?'

It was outrageous, and she got the reaction she expected, even if it was less dramatic than she would have liked. His laugh was one of disbelief. 'You look so innocent sitting there—little shark! Mabye I should have left you to your own devices after all. Supposing I gave you twice what you paid?'

She didn't even need to consider it. He couldn't have much of an idea what the carpet was worth in reality, but once again she was overwhelmed by a desire to see how high she could get him to go if she put her mind to it. He was becoming a sort of professional challenge.

The rest of the ride to the village was passed in intermittent bargaining, with unsatisfactory bursts of conversation. She was cagey about telling him anything of herself as yet. The only piece of information she parted with freely was her name, Zelda Denton. But she parried his enquiries with questions of her own, and discovered disappointingly little from his laconic replies in the process, except that he was from London and English like herself despite his foreign-sounding name—Kalinsky.

'Aram is my first name,' he pointed out with a hint of amusement in that deep, slightly edgy voice. 'You didn't wait for me to explain.'

She gathered that he was in business of some sort, and, having just had a brief holdiay in Syria, was also bound northwards for Turkey the following day.

By the time they reached the village he was heading for, she had got him up to a figure that would give her a disappointing two hundred and seventy-five per cent profit on the Turkish carpet—and then the journey proved to be a wild-goose chase. On the hunt for souvenirs, Aram had heard that this second village also made carpets, but his enquiries in that very authentic-sounding Arabic turned up only one old man with very little to offer.

'Isn't Arabic an unusual language for someone with a name like Kalinsky?' she queried, during a pause in the interview. 'Are you Polish or Russian?'

'Anglo-Polish-French with a bit of Armenian thrown in for good measure. And, no, I don't think so. I learned it at night-school.'

'Why?' she demanded, frankly curious. 'Is it something to do with your job?'

One side of his mouth turned down in an expression that was half disapproval, half humour. 'I thought it might come in useful some time.' And he turned with finality back to the dealer.

It was an obvious brush-off, and Zelda, slightly piqued, surveyed the unimpressive samples of local manufacture with no great interest. Then without thinking she said dismissively, 'There's nothing any good here.'

Her companion looked at her in a way she couldn't quite interpret. 'How do you know?' he asked slowly. 'Some of it's quite attractive.'

Caught out, she wondered if she should reveal her secret there and then. Well, why not? It would let him know that all that bargaining in the car had been nothing more than a game to her. That would put him in his place! He was so damned sure of himself.

The rakish eye-patch was still a little alarming, but she wasn't going to be put off by it. Looking him directly in his one good eye, she announced triumphantly, 'I know because I deal in carpets. That's my job!'

Whatever gratification she was going to get out of it was in the fractional silence that met her announcement, because his subsequent reaction was totally unexpected, and, far from feeling that she had scored, Zelda was thoroughly disconcerted.

He burst out laughing.

CHAPTER TWO

'So what did you find so funny back there?' Zelda demanded, when they were seated in the car again, headed back the way they had come.

Aram was still grinning to himself, and it irritated her. If there was a joke why didn't he share it?

'Oh, just something to do with the fact anyone might take you for a helpless little tourist,' he said offhandedly.

'I don't see that's so hilarious!'

That set him off again. He had a deep, infectious laugh but she felt too annoyed to respond to it. She had wanted revenge for his unwelcome patronage, not paroxysms of mirth at her expense. 'Sorry,' he apologised, eventually, but he didn't sound it. 'It's my warped sense of humour. And your attempt just now to drive another hard bargain with me—another sales ploy?'

'You were the one who suggested buying the thing in the first place!' she pointed out tartly.

He didn't reply for a moment, and then commented, 'So, Zelda, you're a fully fledged carpet dealer, are you? Who do you work for? Someone in England?'

'For myself,' she replied coolly. 'And two friends who run the business with me.'

'And would you say your business was doing well?'

'*Very* well.' The emphasis was a bit overdone, but she wasn't going to have him patronising her, and he'd never find out the truth of anything she was telling him anyway. Besides, now that she'd revealed the fact she was a dealer, there wasn't much point withholding the relevant information. And she felt an overwhelming need to impress him. 'We've got a phenomenal turnover for the size of the company, given that we've only been in existence for just over a year. My partner Melanie Sharman is very good on the business side, and her cousin Richard is wonderful at handling the sales. Of course, we had to take out a massive bank loan to start the whole thing and that's hanging over our heads a bit at the moment, but once we've got past our present cash-flow difficulties we ought to do really well.'

'What makes you so confident? Quite a few small businesses start up with a lot of enthusiasm and then go to pieces through lack of proper management.' He sounded scathing all of a sudden, and Zelda, piqued, turned to him at once.

'So what qualifies you to hand out the advice?' she demanded. 'You don't know the first thing about us!'

He ignored that. 'OK, so you've got a wonderful business manager and a wonderful salesman—what are you wonderful at, Zelda?'

Was he deliberately trying to goad her? His tone of voice suggested that he didn't think she could be particularly remarkable at anything—which was galling when he'd just seen her in action.

'Succeeding!' she said defiantly. 'I've got a lot of older brothers who used to think I was some kind of toy my parents gave them for Christmas. They're still convinced they know better than me—and they don't. That's all.'

'And just how do you propose to prove that to them?' He sounded less sarcastic now—more intrigued.

'"The cunning of a fox and the killer instincts of a shark,"' she announced enigmatically. 'And the shark bit was meant as a compliment that time!'

'I beg your pardon?'

'I was quoting. That's what Rick said about me.'

'And modest with it.'

This time she could see that he was trying, not very successfully, not to laugh again, that hawk face quirking humorously to one side. 'I'm the buyer,' she said as coldly as she could manage. 'And I'm extremely good at negotiating bargains when I don't have to cope with interfering and unscrupulous people like you. So what exactly do *you* do?'

There was a moment's pause. Then, 'I'm a businessman.'

'What sort of business?'

'Buying and selling things—like you.' Getting information out of him was real blood-out-of-a-stone work—and his evasiveness was increasingly suspicious. But, before she had a chance to follow that up, he asked, 'Does your friend Rick handle all the sales, or do you take a turn with the customers when you get back home?'

'I'm strictly a buyer,' she replied shortly. 'Besides, Rick won't let me.'

'Oh?'

She gave an impatient sigh—this was turning into an inquisition. 'Some of the customers are so *stupid*! They might just as well be getting something off a roll in a chain store for all they care about the knots and the dyes—they haven't a clue what they're buying.' That was telling him, and if the cap fitted...! But the only re-action was a lift of dark eyebrow and an expectant pause, so she added, 'I get kind of possessive about my rugs—especially when I think how they started life in an Eastern craftsman's back room in the most romantic circumstances imaginable.'

He glanced at her, and then back at the road. 'So you're a romantic, are you, Zelda?'

'Only about certain aspects of carpet buying!' she flashed defensively. She didn't want him getting ideas...

'Which aspects?'

She shrugged, and turned away from him to stare out into the stony desert, unwilling to part with any more of herself when he was so cagey about returning the compliment.

But he was prepared to wait for an answer, and, goaded by the silence that followed, she found herself saying reluctantly, 'It's the travel... and the unexpected places you find yourself in—one day in a bazaar that smells of spices, the next with a glass of tea in your hand in some dirty little back room out in the wilds, with nothing between you and the mountains but a curtain over the door...'

The pause was unexpectedly filled. 'And the old brigand you're trying to make a deal with has a gun propped up against the wall, and you wonder if it's loaded, which it probably is, and if he's honest... And then, because of the effort involved, and because of the risks, your carpet isn't just a carpet any longer, but something worth more than money to you. Isn't that it, Zelda?'

She looked across at him in astonishment. Yes, it was it. But how did he know?

She had felt there was a sort of bond between them during that bargaining session back at the Arab's, two minds enjoying the same game, but this disconcerted her... It must be clever guesswork. He'd travelled. He might even be as romantic about out-of-the-way places as she was.

Just at that moment he swerved to avoid a pot-hole, causing her to fall against him suddenly. The unexpected contact was so unnerving that she forgot everything except a renewed reluctance to be involved with him any further—it all seemed suddenly to be getting out of her control.

'Did you have to do that?' she demanded defensively, righting herself, and taking an unnecessarily panicky hold of the car seat. Play it cool. You've only got to get to Aleppo. 'Couldn't we go a bit slower? You don't have to handle this thing like a Ferrari just because you haven't got a lower gear.'

She was a little reassured by his smile—it struck her as distinctly patronising, re-establishing some of the familiar antagonism. 'What do you know about driving Ferraris? I bet you couldn't recognise one if it came up and hit you.'

'My eldest brother had one,' she said with acid sweetness. 'I used to drive it.'

That wasn't strictly accurate—Jem had let her handle it once, on a private road, and sweated blood all three miles of the experience. But this wasn't an exercise in truth: it was part of an attempt to set him at a safe psychological distance again.

Aram gave no indication as to whether he believed her or not, but she suspected from the tone of his next question that he didn't. 'How old are you, Zelda?'

'Twenty-three.' She gave the answer grudgingly.

'Older than you look—but still a bit young to be knocking around like this. Are you sure you can take care of yourself in this part of the world?'

'I can handle it,' she said with a cold assurance that clearly surprised him, judging by his expression. He'd made a mistake if he thought that revealing her as a 'romantic' might establish any vulnerability.

'How come you know so much about dealing in rugs?'

She felt her confidence returning. There was no harm in talking about business. She wouldn't be with him for much longer.

'My father used to own salerooms in London. I was always hanging about auctions, and my father's particular interest is in carpets. Two of my brothers—George and Michael, not Jem with the Ferrari—run a couple of antique shops and I used to pick up things for them occasionally.' Her first sincere smile since meeting him was purely one of reminiscence and she was entirely unaware of it, her face lighting up with a sort of wicked delight. 'We're in family competition now—I don't think they like the fact that I can spot a better bargain than they can! But then I specialise.'

He was looking at her, and her involuntary smile evoked an answering one from him. The hawk features seemed less predatory this time. 'How many brothers have you got exactly? You make it sound as though there's a tribe of them.'

She grinned at him directly, unconsciously relaxing a little in response. 'That's just what Dad and I call them—the tribe. I've got four and they're all older than me. My mother died after I was born and I've been brought up in a male-dominated household as a sort of honorary boy—I even went to judo classes with Dominic. He's the next up in age. Perhaps that's why I've never been too worried about "knocking around" in places like this.'

'Black belt?' It *almost* sounded as though he were taking her seriously.

'No,' she admitted with reluctance. 'Not quite. Dom is, though. I suppose martial arts come more naturally to real boys—and he was always quite aggressive.'

Aram glanced across at her again, and she thought he was going to make some comment about her last remark. This time she was aware that his appraisal was a very personal one, but she didn't have time to react.

'What do you mean, "real boys"?' he asked, and there was a new note in his voice—a sort of throaty warmth that was purely animal and made her want to shiver. 'You don't look much like any sort of boy to me.'

She looked at him sideways, with renewed wariness, but for a different reason this time. Aram Kalinsky, eye-patch and all, might really be rather too dangerously attractive. She hadn't seen it at first, not obviously anyway because he wasn't the type she usually went for—tall blond men who never seemed to fall for her. She found herself noting the way that crisp blue-black hair sprung back from a high, intelligent forehead. Yes—definitely the Roman emperor look, she thought, with those fine cheekbones and that aquiline nose. His skin was lightly tanned, and she could see the dark hairs on his chest where his shirt was open at the neck. He looked strong, and he was a great deal taller than she was.

She might have to be careful if she didn't want to find herself involved with this enigmatic character. There was some magnetic quality in him, yes, but he also made her feel very insecure. She still didn't know the first thing about him. And she was no innocent—she knew exactly what the kind of conversation they were now having could lead to. 'You've got a very intriguing profile,' he commented, before she could change the topic. 'With that lovely flat little nose and that sexy mouth.'

'My nose isn't flat!' she protested, her voice splitting suddenly into a husky squeak, piqued by the way he commented on her so frankly. But she wasn't going to argue about the remark on her mouth—Dominic had been fairly blunt about her attributes when, in more naïve and vulnerable days, she'd complained to him tearfully at the end of one particularly disastrous relationship.

'What's the matter with me?' she'd sniffed. 'Every man I go out with seems to have his mind set on only one thing right from the start—we've hardly even said hello before he wants to kiss me, and then once he's done that he thinks it's an invitation to get straight into bed.'

She'd managed to avoid the bed bit up to then.

'It's that sexy pout. If I weren't your brother I'd probably fancy you like mad,' he'd said, examining her with a critical eye, and then added the fraternal put-down. 'I bet you do it on purpose really. And it's a pity you're so flat-chested.'

But being 'so flat-chested' hadn't been as much of a drawback as she might have been led to expect—while she seemed hopelessly drawn to just the sort of men who preferred curvaceous blondes, too many young men in whom she had no interest at all had shown it was precisely that sexy pout of hers that had attracted *them*. They seemed to find that slight fullness of her underlip irresistible.

She could cope with that sort of thing now. In those early days, straight out of the sixth form, she'd found it hard to adjust to being considered as a sex object—which was very much the way she saw it after the easy companionship of her brothers and the mild crushes she'd had on boys at school. She knew now that the dangers lay not in the men who were attracted to her, but in herself—her own tendency to fall headlong in love with someone who didn't necessarily feel the same way about her, and to become too emotionally involved too quickly.

But she'd paid a price for her self-knowledge. Her last and most disastrous romance had been with someone she'd imagined with whole-hearted recklessness she would love for life, and believed he had thought the same way about her—until he'd broken off the relationship a few months later in favour of a former girlfriend. But what made it all so much worse, from her point of view, was that the romance had turned into a full-scale affair and she had felt bound to Dan in a way she had never experienced before.

Well, she wasn't going to let something like that occur again.

She was about to switch the subject very firmly on to more neutral ground when they hit the pot-hole that was to cause her to change every single one of the plans she'd made.

This time she found herself being flung against the door as she was violently bounced from her seat. There was an appalling grinding noise as the car jerked forward, and finally slewed to a halt.

She took a deep breath, rubbing her arm where it had hit the door, and turned to the man beside her. 'What was that?'

'A pot-hole,' he said with such devastating obviousness she almost cringed. The curse that followed was of a quality she'd never even heard from her men at home, as he leaned forward to switch off the ignition and got out.

Without waiting for instructions, she scrambled out at her side, and surveyed the damage.

The situation didn't look promising. There was a thick black slick of oil already oozing from under the car.

She glared at him accusingly. 'You were going too fast! This wouldn't have happened if you'd slowed down—I told you!'

'And I told you why I couldn't go any slower. If you can't think of anything helpful to say, I'd shut up if I were you.'

Zelda was used to being told to shut up, but she wasn't used to taking any notice of it. She opened her mouth to tell him just what she thought of him—stranding them out in the wastes of the Syrian desert—and then caught sight of the look on his face. It wasn't so much the way the dark brows were drawn together in a forbidding frown that stopped her, as that indefinable something about him she had already sensed—that impression he gave of a hidden power simmering away underneath the surface reactions.

Intimidated, she swallowed the retort she was about to make and awaited developments.

He walked a few paces back to the pot-hole that had caused the disaster, and then lay down full length in the stony dirt to peer under the car. It didn't take long for him to reach his conclusions, whatever they were, and he was on his feet again, brushing the dust from his shirt. If she expected an explanation, it wasn't forthcoming.

'So what's the matter with it?' she said at last, braving his displeasure. 'It looks a bit final to me.'

'It is a bit final,' he said brusquely. 'It's the oil sump. The whole thing cracked when we hit that rock in the road coming out of a pot-hole. Without oil the car won't go. I suspect that with the speed it happened, the engine's already seized up.'

'Isn't it worth just trying the ignition to see?' she suggested with heavy patience. After all, it would be stupid to imagine themselves marooned just for the want of a little practical experiment. 'We don't want to be stuck out here unless there's nothing else we can do.'

The look he gave her was withering. 'All right, Miss Ferrari Driver—be my guest.'

He gestured mockingly towards the door, and then leaned back against the side of the bonnet, feet crossed and arms folded.

That told her pretty conclusively he had no doubts about his assessment of the situation, and underneath she was inclined to believe him. But again it was that irritating assumption that he knew better than she did that riled her. Flicking her hair back in a way that was indistinguishable from an arrogant toss of the head, she got into the driver's seat and turned the ignition key. The engine fired once, and then there was a sort of churning sound which died away in a long whine. Then there was silence. She turned the key twice more, pumping at the accelerator with her foot, but there was no further response.

She gave an exasperated sigh. This was all she needed—to be stuck out in the middle of nowhere with an arrogant know-all, when, if only she'd waited in the carpet dealer's village, she'd have got a lift back from Farouq. And she'd like nothing better just at the moment than to take it out on the stupid idiot who hadn't listened to her in the first place. Oh, *why* had she been such a fool as to accept this lift? It wasn't even as though she liked the man—first he had lost her money on a deal— she was still fully convinced that she could have done better at that—and now it was his fault that they wouldn't get back to Aleppo for hours and hours, if they were lucky enough to get back at all! But she wouldn't get anywhere by shouting at him.

Leaning an arm on the roof of the now defunct vehicle, Aram Kalinsky was looking down at her through the open window.

'Well?' he enquired mockingly. 'What's the expert's opinion?'

The deliberate sting in his words destroyed all her intentions of exercising self-control. 'I don't know why you imagine you're in a position to be sarcastic about it!' she blazed at him. 'It's your fault. You shouldn't have been driving so fast on this road—it was perfectly obvious! So what if we'd crawled along in second gear? At least we'd have got back eventually! Now we could be here for hours and hours. I'm supposed to be leaving for Turkey tomorrow and I haven't even arranged a lift yet!'

'Calm down.' He sounded exasperatingly cool in contrast to her fury. 'I'm a little bored with the subject of my driving. If you think you can do any better, you're welcome to try next time.'

'There won't be a next time if I can help it!' she retorted quickly.

'Oh? Then you wouldn't accept a lift into Turkey tomorrow if I offered you one?'

She glared at him. 'How can you offer me a lift when you don't have a car to drive any longer? This is hardly a little matter of ringing up your local garage, is it?'

He shrugged. 'It's up to you. I'll be hiring another car in Aleppo. There's no way I'd have taken this one anyway, and, now you've finished off the engine, it's only just about fit for scrap.'

'What do you mean, *I've* finished off the engine?' she demanded. Really, he was impossible!

'You only succeeded in doing what I'd thought had happened already,' he replied dismissively. 'But you don't have to take that as a premeditated insult.'

He was studying her again, but a quick glance at his impassive expression told her nothing. She chewed her bottom lip angrily. She didn't want to accept another lift with him if she could help it, but she definitely didn't want to hang around in Aleppo any longer either. The city was fascinating, but there were few tourists and she found some of the treatment she met with, being a young European woman on her own, very tiresome. And she had a plane to catch in Istanbul.

'Is that a serious offer of a lift?' She'd made up her mind to refuse it straight off if he came out with one more aggressive comment.

'It is. Do you want to accept it?'

On the other side of the open window like that, the strong hawk-like features were disconcertingly close to her own. She found herself studying the fine lines at the corner of his eye, the strongly defined cheekbones, and determined mouth now twisted in a slight smile. His being so close did something to her insides. She found herself breathing a little faster, almost as though... Perhaps it wouldn't be such a good idea after all. 'Can I think about it?' she asked quickly.

He shrugged. 'OK. But don't think too long. I'm definitely leaving one way or another tomorrow. I've got business in Konya coming up in a few days.'

'So what are we going to do now?'

The answer to that was simple—wait. He reminded her that her friend Farouq would probably be returning along their route, since he had agreed to pick her up at the dealer's and wouldn't know about the change of plans. They were probably only a few miles from the village as it was.

'Couldn't we walk to it?' she pleaded. Sitting there indefinitely with him was, for reasons she didn't examine, getting to be an unnerving prospect.

'No way.' He dismissed it immediately. 'You should know that you never leave your car in the desert—wandering off on foot is the worst thing you could do.'

'But we're on a main road and this isn't exactly the blazing Saharan sands, is it?' she argued. The stony Syrian desert in October was no more than warm during the day, although it could get very chilly at night.

'Some main road.' His reply was heavy with sarcasm. He opened the door beside her. 'Move over. I might as well sit in here. It could be a long wait.'

She was no longer very keen on the proximity, now that there was nothing to occupy them but each other, but since she was determined not to sit there in hostile silence they chatted for a while. Most of the contributions were made by her, but it emerged after a while

that her companion was extensively travelled in the
Middle East. He was well informed about the area they
were in, and his comments, though brief, were interesting. She wished he'd volunteer the information more
willingly, but even so the minutes would have ticked past
too slowly for her. She was growing impatient with the
fruitless waiting, and very thirsty. It was close to sunset,
and the pleasant warmth of the day had begun to fade.

After a while she got out her book and tried to read,
but the plot failed to hold her interest, and she was just
about to give it up as a bad job when the tall man beside
her moved abruptly and got out. She glanced up quickly,
and, with the car sideways to the road, had a good view
in both directions. To her left, in the distance, were two
tiny pinpricks of light in the rapidly thickening dusk—
headlamps.

She jumped out and joined him instantly, waving her
arms instinctively even though at that distance it was
unlikely that she would be clearly seen.

'Hey! Hey, stop!' she yelled, in an agony of suspense,
and turned to Aram desperately. 'Supposing he doesn't
see us?' Her companion gave a derisive snort. 'What—
with the car halfway across his road, and you jumping
about like a demented puppet? Save your voice for
later—you might need it for something.'

She shot him a furious look—he really did have a sarcastic sense of humour—and then focused her attention
on the approaching vehicle.

It turned out to be a battered Range Rover, piled high
with old oil cans, mattresses, cardboard boxes, and as-
sorted household objects that suggested primitive re-
movals. Its roof, equally stacked, was covered with an
old tarpaulin. Even the front seat was littered with objects. It was driven by a Syrian in European dress, who
stopped immediately.

All the negotiations were carried out in Arabic by
Aram—and Zelda couldn't follow one word of them.
For all she knew, he might have been offering to sell her

in exchange for the lift. She resented the fact that she
had to put herself into his hands so completely—and it
wasn't just the fact that she wasn't used to depending
on somebody else that annoyed her—but in the circumstances she had no alternative.

'OK,' he said at last 'Hop in. This guy's going to take
us back to Aleppo.'

It was easier said than done, and involved lengthy
rearrangements on the part of the Syrian. He grinned at
Zelda, gesturing to the front seat, and with difficulty
proceeded to clear a space. Her two carpets were pushed
in among the other household goods, and at that point
it became obvious that there was not one further inch .
of room to be made in the entire vehicle.

She clambered up into the space the Syrian had indicated, shifting over towards the centre as far as she
could. It had just occurred to her that that wasn't really
going to leave much of a seat for another body—and
one considerably larger than hers—when she felt herself
being caught up in a pair of strong arms and swung,
helpless to resist, out of the Range Rover again.

'Oh, no, you don't! We're getting out of this
together—even if you do feel like leaving me stranded
for driving you into pot-holes!' The tone of the deep
voice this time was distinctly teasing, but for one
breathless moment she couldn't think of a reply. The
sensation of being held in this man's arms was so unexpected she could do nothing but gaze up at him in
startled dismay, one arm clutched instinctively across the
broad muscular shoulders. It was suddenly as though
every inch of her body that had come into contact with
his were being scorched, but in a most extraordinary
way—it made her want to shiver. She was so close to
him she could smell a lingering tang of aftershave, and
see the pores of his skin. There was an underlying
darkness along his jaw that etched in a new growth of
beard.

Half crushed against him, she searched desperately for some answering comment—any comment—her lips parting to stammer out some reply, and then, as she registered the sudden increase of tension in the body that held hers, there was a moment of absolute stillness.

As they stared at each other in that suspended moment, the image of a hawk—predatory, hovering above his prey—flashed through her mind. For one split second she was aware of what he was going to do. But she had no time to think—nor to react. The kiss was so swift it was over almost before it had begun, but it had an effect on her that she was totally unprepared for. As though stars were exploding somewhere inside her, or a sudden electric charge had shot right through her blood, everything for a couple of seconds was completely blotted out but the sensation evoked by that predatory mouth on hers.

Then, before she was fully conscious of what was happening, he had set her quickly on her feet, and was in the seat she had occupied only seconds before, pulling her up on to his knee. She felt completely dazed. Her heart was thudding as though she had just run a four-minute mile, and she didn't dare speculate on what the Syrian must be thinking—or on what had prompted such a response from her enigmatic companion. And, as for her own reactions to what had just happened, she couldn't find any coherent thoughts at all...

The ride back was memorably uncomfortable, though the awkwardness had less to do with the cramped conditions than with the way in which she was forced to sit, her legs almost twined with Aram's in order to avoid the gear-stick, and one arm round his neck to enable her to keep a stable position. She was aware of the muscles of the strong thighs under her own, and she felt as though his hand, resting on the curve of her waist, was almost burning a hole through the thin cotton of her loose trousers. It was easy enough not to look at him directly, but she couldn't help wondering what he was thinking.

Aleppo now seemed like the other side of the world. She couldn't wait to get safely back to her hotel.

Aram kept up a conversation with the Syrian, and she was grateful to him for ignoring her. As for the kiss, it would be best dismissed as something that had happened on the spur of the moment, and forgotten about. Though that was easier said than done when every new pot-hole jolted her more intimately against him.

It was long dark by the time they got to Aleppo. The Syrian was prepared to drop her at her hotel—encouraged, she guessed, by Aram, for which she was grateful. She hadn't relished the idea of looking for a taxi at that time of night.

Aram got out with her, thanking the Syrian on behalf of them both, and some money exchanged hands. Then the tail-lights of their rescuer disappeared down the narrow, poorly lit street.

'Did he expect you to pay him?' she asked awkwardly. That would put her in his debt, if the Arab had gone out of his way on her account.

'No.' The reply was curt, and he offered no further explanation.

Now that they were left face to face on the pavement, she didn't quite know what to say. He was a real mystery man as far as she was concerned. He had told her virtually nothing about himself. A complete stranger— someone she'd met only a few hours ago—and yet that kiss, even though she was keen to forget it, had changed things.

'What are you going to do now? You're not staying at this hotel,' she said, more out of politeness than curiosity. There was a careful pause, and then the white even teeth showed again in a disconcerting smile as he looked down at her.

'Take you out to supper?'

It was the last thing she'd expected. Her heart semeed to give a surprised flip in her chest, before she decided that it was really a bad idea... Maybe he felt he owed it to her for the business over the car; it might even be his way of admitting he had been wrong to speed along like that. But no. Looking at him, she suspected that, far from apologising, he would never see it as an error of judgement in the first place. And now there was the business of tomorrow to sort out. She still wasn't sure what to do about the lift.

'Thanks—but I really am tired,' she said quickly. 'I'll get something to eat here, and I want to ask the manager if he knows anyone who'll be going across the border tomorrow.'

'Why? The offer of the lift still holds.'

'Thanks,' she said again, 'but...' And then she couldn't think of any good reason why she shouldn't accept.

He was watching her critically, his face shadowy and somehow more predatory than ever in the poor light.

'I'll give you the number of my hotel. I'm coming in with you to use the phone for a taxi—I'll write it down inside. If you change your mind, ring me before ten.'

There was only a small foyer, with a high desk for the receptionist who was more often than not the manager. Zelda had stayed there once before, on the recommendation of a friend, which accounted for the trust she was inclined to place in the manager's arrangements.

He greeted her in a friendly way, joking about the elderly Farouq and his readiness to take young women out into the desert, but when she enquired about the possibility of finding a lift to the border the next day he seemed doubtful.

'Maybe the next day—maybe three days,' he said, shaking his head. 'But tomorrow, no. I have not heard of anyone already and it is not much time.'

His glance had lighted curiously on Aram once or twice, and she felt obliged to introduce him.

'I've offered her a lift but she won't take it,' her companion said, grinning.

The manager threw up his hands theatrically. 'But why are you asking me to get you a lift when you have a chauffeur?' he demanded. 'Here you are—this gentleman will call for you tomorrow at the hotel. You only have to step into his car and he will drive you all the way to Istanbul!'

The last comment was clearly added as a joke, but Aram, his arms full of her carpets, made an unexpected reply.

'As a matter of fact I will, if that's what you want.' She examined him suspiciously. 'But you told me earlier you were going to Konya!'

'I am,' he replied quietly. 'And then I'm going on to Istanbul.'

She was torn between the ease with which her travel problems could be sorted out if she accepted a lift with this man, and the sudden irrational conviction that behind his offer lay some sort of deliberate pursuit. First his unwelcome interference in her affairs in the desert village—and why on earth had she accepted a lift she didn't really want when she was already sure of getting back to Aleppo? Then there was the way he continually questioned her while revealing virtually nothing of his own life—and his interest in her hadn't even seemed like the obvious sexual attraction until he had kissed her... And now another lift, one that could keep her in his company for a couple of days at least if she took it...

There was another one of those loaded silences while they looked at each other. This time it was her friend the manager who broke in.

'There you are!' he exclaimed triumphantly. 'I was right! You will get home very safe now, and then maybe I see you again in a few months—who knows?'

Who knows, indeed! she told herself nervously. And as for getting home safe, well... she would get home all right, but she wasn't so sure about the rest of it. For reasons that weren't the obvious ones, and for reasons she wasn't even sure she could define to herself as yet, 'safe' wasn't a word she'd have chosen to use in the context of Aram Kalinsky.

CHAPTER THREE

IT HAD been a male conspiracy, Zelda decided the next day, sitting a little apprehensively in the foyer waiting for Aram to appear. With the two of them against her, there hadn't been much she could do in the end but agree to what sounded like an ideal offer. She knew very little about her mysterious companion, and she wasn't sure she could trust him, but what could she honestly object to apart from the fact that he had kissed her?

She had lain awake for a long time during the night, wondering if she wasn't doing something very stupid indeed. But she had never got into any scrape in the past that she hadn't been able to get out of, and her confidence in her own quick wits went a long way to persuade her that there wasn't really much to worry about. She could leave him at the border, if she didn't like the look of the way things were going.

Then, the moment he appeared, she was aware once again of that indefinable quality about him—that aura she felt sure would set him apart from every other man in a room. He was dressed in a casual shirt and a pair of well-pressed light-coloured trousers, and the instant he stepped inside the little hotel foyer he seemed to fill it. She had been on edge about this meeting from the moment she had got out of bed. She was still in two minds about going at all.

'Ready?' he asked, with that flash of a smile that somehow made him look so foreign—it was hard to believe that he really was English.

She indicated the heap of baggage waiting by the desk. It was something she had omitted to mention to him the night before.

44

'I'm afraid there are a few things I've got to take with me.' She hoped it would put him off—and that would make up her mind for her.

'How do you intend to get home with all that?' His tone was uncompromising. 'It looks as though you've been buying up half Syria.'

'I have been here nearly a month!' she defended herself. 'It's not such a lot when you think how much time I've had to put into getting it together. Anyway, I told you I was a carpet dealer. What did you expect? And I've only got to get it across the Turkish border and then a friend will deal with it.'

If he made the slightest difficulty, she wouldn't even wait to argue with him, but he merely began to transfer the bags to the car. She assisted, half-heartedly.

The model he had hired looked an improvement on the first, but to her surprise she found that the boot wouldn't open when she went round to pile in her luggage.

'I think I've just found out what's wrong with this one!' she announced. 'I am assuming, of course, that you've already tried out all the gears.'

'Pack your stuff in the back,' he told her, opening one of the passenger doors. 'I've got my things in there.'

Her collection of carpets safely stacked away on the back seat, it did occur to her to wonder what her companion could have been doing to need the entire boot to himself, but the information wasn't forthcoming when she enquired later, as they drove north towards the border.

'I've been in this area for a while and picked up quite a bit,' was all he'd say in answer to her question. 'Is your stuff *all* carpets?'

He indicated the bags piled in the back. Some of them were just canvas-wrapped bundles, and others were tied with rope. There was only one light holdall that represented her personal luggage.

'Most of it. I've only got to get it as far as Malatya. A Turkish friend of mine helps with it. I've been in Asia for over two months now, buying carpets. I usually get the stuff to Mehmet, and he arranges for it to hitch a lift with friends who are driving through to Europe. If I'm going home, I take a few rugs on to the plane.'

'Is this Mehmet part of your business too?' His interest sounded genuine.

'Well, sort of. He handles just the transfer arrangements, and gets a small cut of the profits we make on the stuff he sends back to England. It's annoying really.' She launched into her favourite grievance. 'We could make so much more money if there was someone else doing my job as well as me. Mehmet could cope with double the work he gets from us, and we sometimes sell what we've bought so fast that there's a real problem with supply and demand. It's just that the way we have to do it—with only two people in England working flat out, and me out here a lot of the time—makes everything take so long and cost so much more.'

He gave her one of those keen glances. 'So you think you've got a good business going if only you could expand?'

She nodded. 'Yes, I do. We've done amazingly well up to now. My father was pretty sceptical about it, and Melanie's father thought we'd be bankrupt in a month. But we've got our own warehouse, and we sell to other retailers as well as directly to individual customers. We've got a good turnover, but we need more capital, and we've already taken out that big bank loan. It's a catch-22 situation: we can't take on more people until we make more money, and we can't make more money until we take on more people.'

'Ever thought of asking someone to back you, in exchange for a share of the increased profits?'

'I don't suppose we have very seriously,' she said gloomily. 'Melanie mostly handles the financial side, and she's afraid of taking on a debt we won't be able to meet.

Rick always supports her, and they both think I'm too reckless.'

'So you'd consider it if the right offer came along?'

She laughed. 'I'd consider anything if the right offer came along!'

He gave her a sideways look. 'I'll remember that.'

From the tone of his voice it was obvious he didn't just have carpets in mind, and she regretted her off-the-cuff remark. But then, to her relief, he said, 'Supposing I give you three and a half times as much as you paid for that rug you bought yesterday—will you sell it? That's an unrepeatable offer.'

It was the sum she'd mentioned the day before in the mock bargaining session, but she hadn't been serious. 'Nope. Mention four and a half, and we might start talking.'

He looked amused, and she found she liked the way the side of his mouth quirked, creasing a line of humour into that lean cheek. It made him look less hawk-like.

'You're a greedy little negotiator, aren't you?' he was saying. 'You want blood with it! No deal. It's only quite a pretty rug, after all. I thought I was doing you a favour—you'd be making a big profit, and you wouldn't have to go to all the trouble of getting it home.'

'You don't know the first thing about carpets,' she said smugly. 'I'm not selling.'

He shrugged in that characteristic laconic manner. 'You'd better hope you won't regret this.'

'I won't.'

The drive to the border didn't offer much of interest, particularly to someone who had travelled the route several times before as Zelda had done. The land was flat and poor, and the road increasingly occupied by heavy lorries heading in both directions. They passed a military check-point, where both their passports were carefully scrutinised—Aram's particularly, despite its familiar British insignia.

'I'm not surprised,' Zelda remarked, as they drove on again. 'You don't look in the least bit English, and your name certainly isn't. How do you come to be posing as a Britisher?'

'It's not a pose. I was born and brought up in London. My grandfather was Polish but he left home when he was a boy. He lived first in Paris, where he started a business, and then, when he met my Armenian grandmother, moved to London. I'm supposed to resemble her side of the family. My mother was English, if that's any help.'

'Are your parents still alive?'

'No, but I've got a vast network of Franco-Polish-Armenian relations—and one sister.'

It sounded a romantic ancestry, and was in keeping with his appearance. 'You still look very exotic despite your English mother,' she said frankly. 'But I suppose it might have something to do with your eye-patch.'

'I suppose it might,' he said unhelpfully.

Her curiosity about the patch had been growing ever since she had first seen him. She had felt to begin with that it might be tactless to enquire about it—perhaps he had lost an eye in some terrible accident—but she was morbidly fascinated by it. With that hooked nose and his strong features he looked like some medieval corsair, or predatory Arabian prince.

Then something that had been niggling at her ever since she had started out from Aleppo suddenly occurred to her in a very sinister light indeed... Supposing he *had* lost an eye in an accident—supposing he had been shot at or something! She didn't really know the first thing about him. OK, so he'd explained his passport, but the details weren't reassuring. He could have all sorts of unorthodox foreign connections in this part of the world, and he might be involved in any sort of illegal activity—why had he locked the boot of the car?

Drugs—weapons... he could have anything in there! Would they automatically check it when they went across the border? He had said he was in business, but that could mean anything! They were on the borders of some notorious trouble-spots. He could be gun-running for all she knew. He could even be a terrorist...

Why on earth had she let herself be persuaded into accompanying him? What a fool she'd been! He could even be using her as a cover for whatever it was he was up to; he could tell the authorities whatever he liked about his relationship with her if he spoke to them in Arabic, and she would never know. He had heaped up all her carpets very ostentatiously in the back of the car, and the border officials might assume that the boot was full of the same sort of thing. And if he *was* involved in anything shady, he would be sure to make his activities appear legitimate.

Now she had let her imagination loose, she could almost convince herself that she was in all kinds of trouble. By the time she had explored some of the possibilities, in an intense silence that in itself could arouse his suspicions, she was more than half certain that the boot contained caches of guns and grenades, and that, if Aram Kalinsky wasn't exactly a terrorist himself, he must certainly be involved in questionable paramilitary activity. Just because he had seemed to appreciate the romance of carpet buying and had a winning smile didn't mean he wasn't also unscrupulous and dishonest...

Her heart beating fast, she took a deep breath and came to a swift decision: she would escape his clutches by insisting on hitching a lift with one of the north-bound lorry drivers at the border. She had done it before when she hadn't had a car. Meanwhile, she'd have to act as though everything were normal.

But her companion had noticed the deep, careful breath—he seemed almost suspiciously aware of everything about her—and glanced across at her.

'Bored—or tired?' he asked.

'This isn't exactly a fascinating road, is it?' She managed a convincingly offhand tone.

'That depends on your companion.'

'Yes. It does, doesn't it?'

The smart reply made him laugh, but he didn't rise to it, his attention claimed by the traffic ahead of them.

At the border, however, things didn't go quite as she had expected. There was the usual long queue of lorries waiting to go through the check-point, and then the shorter tail-back for private vehicles. Aram joined neither of them. Instead, he parked beside the road at some distance from the second queue, and turned to her, resting one strongly muscled arm along the back of her seat in a way that made her acutely aware once again of his physical proximity.

'There's one aspect to this that I hadn't got around to explaining before we left.' Her heart gave an ominous thud: surely he wasn't going to *admit* to being involved in some criminal activity? 'I couldn't manage to get hold of a hired car I could take across the border.'

Such overwhelming relief flooded through her that she was afraid he might be able to see it. 'You mean we have to walk?' she asked—this was a heaven-sent opportunity to part company without its appearing in the least suspicious!

'No. I thought we'd hitch a lift with one of the truckers, and I'll pick up another car at the first suitable town we come to in Turkey. This one's being collected this afternoon by some friend of the guy who rented it to me.'

In other circumstances, she might have felt annoyed that someone who was professing to be offering her a trouble-free lift was actually expecting her to hitch part of the way, but all Zelda felt now was an ecstatic sense of deliverance.

'Don't worry,' she said quickly. 'I'll make my own way from here—I've done it before. I might even find a driver who's going to Malatya. I'll ask along the trucks.'

'Why hitch a lift on your own when you're better off with me?' he demanded. 'I'm going to Istanbul. I've already told you. I'd be glad of the company.'

'You could pick up another hitch-hiker.'

'OK. I'd be glad of *your* company, Zelda.'

She returned his direct look warily. She wasn't sure she could read his expression—it seemed to challenge her and she wondered if he had guessed she was keen to get away from him, but that didn't fully account for it. Then, before she could say anything else, he was out of the car, and heading for the line of lorries all waiting for clearance to cross the border. Many of the drivers had got out of their trucks, and had joined others to smoke and chat, used to the long delays.

She watched the mysterious Aram with his long stride moving quickly among them, but before she had made up her mind what to do he was heading back to the car again.

'There's a guy with a virtually empty truck near the top of the queue who'll take us baggage and all. He's going to Malatya, which is just what you wanted. And it shouldn't be too difficult to hire a car there.'

Zelda considered him, making up her mind. If he was prepared to put the contents of the boot into the back of a lorry that would surely be checked, then he couldn't be too worried about it. But, on the other hand, if the lorry was officially empty, they mightn't bother...

'Isn't there anyone going to Istanbul?' she asked quickly, even though a direct lift wouldn't be much use to her. Since there was no way she could take so many carpets home with her, she would have to see Mehmet, but she needn't tell Aram that.

'Yes. Me,' he said firmly. 'Don't get out. I'll queue-jump and then we can load all the baggage directly into the truck. I've got to go in and have a word with the border guards about where to leave this anyway.'

Through indecision, she lost her opportunity to make any immediate changes to his plans. He seemed deter-

mined to keep her with him—which might give some
substance to the suspicion that he was using her as
cover—and she was angry with herself for letting it
happen. She didn't usually have such difficulty in making
a clear-cut decision about something—or somebody.
Never mind, she consoled herself, with the lorry driver
for company she couldn't come to any harm, and she'd
get rid of her potential terrorist once and for all when
she'd contacted Mehmet.

The boot of the hired car proved to contain several
large boxes, which were swiftly loaded into the back of
the lorry by Aram. He gave no hint as to what they contained, even when she asked him directly.

'Merchandise,' he said succinctly, and ignored her
subsequent enquiry, turning to the driver to whom he
spoke in Turkish. She caught the word 'carpets' and then
her own bundles were heaped into the back. The driver,
a mustachioed Turk with humorous brown eyes, didn't
seem worried by Aram's mysterious crates and the two
soon engaged in a rapid conversation which Zelda, with
her smattering of Turkish, was unable to follow.

As before when they had been stuck in the desert with
the car, it unnerved her that her companion was able to
communicate so fluently without her understanding. It
made her feel unusually vulnerable.

He must have seen her expression of doubt. 'Don't
worry. You'll get to Istanbul.'

He had misinterpreted the cause of her anxiety, but
she took advantage of it. 'Yes, but I've got a flight to
catch and I'm already booked on to it—I can't afford
to miss it!' She had, in fact, several days in hand, but
she wasn't going to tell him that. It was her best excuse
for getting out of his clutches.

'How long have you got?'

'Er—about three days,' she said quickly.

He was studying her again now in that disconcerting
way of his, but merely gave a lift of one dark eyebrow.

'You'll get there in time,' he said.

She stared back, about to argue further, and then he gave her one of those unexpected dazzling smiles that made her want to smile back and weakly go along with anything he suggested.

Crossing the border was never quick. There was all the official business to be gone through first on the Syrian side, and then on the Turkish, before they could head north for Malatya, over one hundred and fifty miles away. It might be several hours' drive and very late to contact Mehmet when she arrived. Still, she could off-load the bulk of the carpets the next day, and with any luck Mehmet could arrange a trouble-free lift for her at least to Ankara, if not all the way to Isanbul. As a last resort, she could always catch long-distance buses.

She spent some of the time while they waited playing cards with a Scottish lorry driver in the cab behind her. It was a relief to find someone who spoke the same language, and, by the time they parted, she was genuinely sorry he wasn't going her way. They had got on very well over the bottle of whisky he produced from under the seat. Zelda hadn't drunk very much, but it had cheered her up a bit.

'You smell like a distillery,' Aram accused, with a surprised look when she reappeared in the Turkish driver's cab.

She didn't know if it was the drink affecting her judgement, but he didn't seem quite so sinister as she clambered up beside him.

'You're just jealous!' she said pertly.

'Too right I am! Next time you find such a hospitable trucker, invite me along too.' He was looking amsued, and caught her eye.

She still didn't know if it was the drink affecting her, but she suddenly found herself thinking that it was a pity she had so many doubts about him—he was such an attractive man. And then she remembered that un-expected kiss in the desert. It must have been a very fleeting impulse on his part, because despite his interest in keeping her with him he hadn't tried to repeat it. And she found herself wishing that he would. Right now. And take rather longer about it this time...

But she was determined to give away none of the peculiar physical effects he was having on her—the most ominous being a sort of melting weakness inside that she identified from bitter experience and tried to ignore.

'You can't blame me,' she said defensively. 'You never made the slightest effort to translate any of your conversation for me.'

He shrugged. 'I didn't think you'd be interested in discussing the economics of tea plantation east of Trabzon. My mistake.'

The tone of his reply sounded characteristically cutting, and she couldn't tell whether he was teasing or serious. Zelda was used to having the last word, but it wasn't so easy with this man. She thought better of making a clever retort, and subsided, the warm little glow very definitely wearing off. She couldn't help feeling disappointed. It must have been the whisky.

They made one stop before Malatya, at a small roadside restaurant where their driver had some business to discuss with a friend. Zelda was glad of the chance to stretch her legs and freshen up, and she was also hungry. It was hours since breakfast in the hotel in Aleppo.

She had been right in her assessment of Aram in one respect at least—he was the sort of man who invariably drew the attention of the people around him. Despite his occasionally rather withdrawn manner towards Zelda herself, he quickly got involved in conversation with the café patrons, and it wasn't long before he was seated at one of the tables with several locals, and two other lorry drivers, involved in a game of cards. When Zelda reappeared from the ladies' he gestured to an empty chair beside him.

'Play poker?' he enquired, the quizzical lift of one eyebrow suggesting that he was almost certain she didn't.

She knew very well this was his way of showing her that he had been right not to include her earlier—there really wouldn't be much she could contribute.

But fate had rewarded her for her earlier forbearance, and given her a much more satisfactory opportunity of scoring. She hadn't been brought up with four unscrupulous card players, all older than herself, without learning a thing or two!

'Of course,' she said nonchalantly, and took her place beside him. She could tell by the expression on that hawk-like face that he was surprised, and still sceptical.

Typically, there were no other women in the café, and Zelda quickly attracted a great deal of notice. There was a certain amount of good-natured humour—with her inadequate Turkish she couldn't understand any of it, and Aram declined to translate, but she was pretty sure that she was the object of it. It didn't disconcert her in the least. Her own rather unusual background had given her a lot of confidence, and since her early childhood, as the devastatingly pretty baby sister of no less than three doting older brothers—Dominic, nearest in age, had been more of a rival—she had been used to being the centre of attention. In addition, she was a very fair hand at poker. Bluff was, after all, a vital ingredient in carpet dealing. She quickly began to win far more than she lost, and it gave her a certain private satisfaction that she had succeeded in stealing the limelight from Aram.

She knew he was watching her out of the corner of his good eye, giving nothing away himself, and she was almost overwhelmingly aware of him in a way that had nothing to do with cards all through the game. They were playing for Turkish lira, but with the low value of the currency she wasn't likely to lose a fortune. She found that with a little bit of luck on her side she was more than a match for the Turkish players—or perhaps they were just amused to observe the struggle developing between herself and Aram. Gradually they dropped out until the game was between just the two of them. She was determined to beat him, and time after time met his expressionless gaze with an equally blank look of her own, as one tried to assess the other's hand.

'Sure you can afford to go on?' she challenged, indicating the little heap of coins and notes in the centre of the table, her eyes sparking in a way that amounted to open flirtation, although she was unaware of it.

He met her look, a half-smile etching the humour each side of his mouth, and his answer was disconcerting. 'I always even up the score in the end—are *you* sure you can afford to *win*?' There was a hint of something in that deep voice that made her repress a little shiver— but it wasn't anything like fear that had prompted it.

They had been playing for nearly an hour, before he suddenly declared defeat. As she raked in her winnings, she couldn't resist a grin of triumph in his direction. He gave her a wry smile, again holding her eyes, but said nothing. There was an infinitesimal pause, as though some invisible balance had shifted. Suddenly awkward, she ignored him and offered to buy all the other players a drink. There was some laughter, and applause, but they insisted that she should accept something from them and that odd moment was lost in the elation at the outcome of the game.

While there was still no sign of the lorry driver, she became aware of a certain amount of banter going on between Aram and their Turkish companions as she slowly sipped her way along the line of tea glasses in front of her—the only drinks she would agree to take. Aram eventually turned to her, and there was one of those expressions on his face that it was impossible to interpret. It occurred to her that he might have been secretly annoyed to have been beaten by a woman in such company, and she still couldn't be sure if it was that wretched eye-patch that was making him appear so enigmatic.

'They want to play a game.'

'What sort of game?' she asked, carefully. 'More cards?'

He gave an amused grin. '*What* a rapacious little girl you are—be satisfied with what you've got!'

She didn't much like that 'little girl'—it was too patronising by half—but she attributed it to pique at having lost to her. And it was a relief to see him smile.

'A game with string,' he said. 'Stand up.'

She didn't really mind what sort of game it was. It would be only until their driver reappeared, and she was quite happy to entertain them all for a bit longer.

She had to admit to herself afterwards that being in the limelight during the poker game must have gone to her head, but even then if she had known what the string involved she would never have agreed to it.

A long piece of twine was produced by the café owner, and tied to each of her wrists. A second was tied to Aram's in the same way, only being looped through her string first. The strings were long enough for them to move some distance from each other, but they could not free themselves without a manoeuvre that involved them getting close together and climbing in and out of the loops. It looked as though it ought to be simple—they weren't linked by any complicated knots—but Zelda suddenly felt extremely reluctant to get anywhere near Aram. If she had imagined she was going to find the same sort of harmless amusement in this that she would have had in playing the game with friends at home, then she had made a serious mistake. The sheer physical proximity of that well-built masculine frame was making her unaccountably nervous.

'I'm assured that it's possible to do this,' he said, a speculative gleam in his eye. 'Shall we find out?' It was obvious that unless they approached each other, and worked out logically whatever that apparently simple manoeuvre was that would free them, they would remain indefinitely tied together.

Trying to hide her dismay, Zelda stared at the string in silence. She was determined to work it out *before* they got too intimately entangled—an event which, of course, the Turks were all eagerly awaiting. It was disconcerting to note that Aram didn't look particularly worried about it either.

The moment she had realised what was involved, an all too vivid recollection of her experiences in his arms the day before had come to her. She didn't want any sort of repeat of that—and especially not in such interested company.

Aram approached her, tall and long-legged, and stood over her, grinning. He reminded her in every way of some handsome brigand out of an old movie.

'Well?' he demanded. 'Got any suggestions?'

Trying to ignore the sensations that dangerous presence was producing in her, she took a step back.

'Wait!' she said quickly—too quickly; it betrayed her nervousness and provoked laughter from her Turkish audience. She pulled herself together and added more coolly, 'Don't let's get tangled up in this—I'm sure there must be a simple way out!'

The Turks were loudly enjoying themselves, and she caught sight of the lorry driver emerging from the back of the serving area with his friend to join the circle that was now round herself and Aram. They were providing a floor show for the entire café. She was regretting her earlier willingness to try to eclipse Aram. This was beginning to look like revenge—what he had meant perhaps by evening the score?

If she took too long about it, the audience would derive even more entertainment from her obvious reluctance to get herself involved with her companion. With one hasty glance at the linking strings, she concluded that the easiest way out was for one of them to stand behind the other, and for the one in front to climb through the strings so that the two would no longer be looped together.

'I'm sure it's the way!' she told Aram with a confidence she was far from feeling. Still, it *looked* possible.

Without speaking, he came to stand behind her. Prickles suddenly stood up all the way down her spine. There were inches still between them, but it was the same as if he had touched her. Involuntarily, she moved a step away from him, and then had to make it look as though she was preparing for the next move.

Stepping through the strings, far from releasing them as she had hoped, merely made a tangle that it was going to be harder to get out of, and, what was worse, the shortened length of twine brought them even closer together.

Aram was grinning down at her. 'That wasn't so successful, was it?' he teased. 'Why don't I try stepping through this time?'

She was about to protest she knew a better way, but he was already getting into some new manoeuvre that ended up with them in even worse confusion. She was only just managing to keep any sort of distance between them. As it was, he was far too close for comfort.

From then on, things went from bad to worse. Although she was sure he was deliberately confusing it, she couldn't accuse Aram directly because all his suggestions seemed reasonable at the time, and she couldn't offer any better ideas herself. But as the strings became more and more entangled and the room for manoeuvre less and less, she found herself virtually in his arms, unable to avoid coming into contact with some part of his body with every movement. The Turks were delighted. They laughed and offered Aram helpful hints at every turn, but she was sure, from the audience reception they got, that the suggestions didn't have much to do with escape.

'Why don't you let me move your arm through this loop here?' Aram was saying.

She was standing facing him, her feet virtually between his, trying to keep her legs and hips from touching him. Without waiting for her reply, he took hold of her arm, as though to operate her body like some sort of marionette, and once again it was just as though his hand had scorched her, even through the loose sweatshirt she was wearing.

With a little gasp, she snatched her arm away, and as she registered the look of surprise on his face, there was an awkward pause. Every single inch of her was aware of that strongly muscled male body so close to hers. It was a purely animal sensation, but stronger than anything she had ever felt in her life. She stared at him, caught up helplessly in that peculiar moment, her breasts rising and falling quickly with every uneven breath. She was aware that he too was breathing faster, and looking down at her with a curious expression.

Then he said, so low that she could only just catch the words, 'Let's get out of this.'

She didn't know what would have happened, if he hadn't abruptly made the move that was to free them. They were quite close to the table at which they had originally been sitting, and where some of the Turks still sat with their drinks, wreathed in the pungent smoke of their cigarettes. Without warning, Aram leaned forward towards one member of their audience. His unexpected movement caused Zelda to shift her weight, and he caught her against him as she overbalanced. She gave a little squeak as her body came into full contact with his, and then she was free—he was stripping away the web that they had created round themselves.

Aware of a sharp smell of burning, she looked down sideways to see that he had a small cigarette lighter in his hand. The blackened ends of a couple of bits of string told all the rest.

Their Turkish audience laughed and clapped, and there were plenty of remarks for Aram, who gave a fleeting smile, and nodded to their forgotten truck driver.

He looked down at Zelda, still standing beside him and at a loss as to what to do next. The unexpected way the game had turned out had deprived her of all initiative. A few seconds was all it had taken—and everything seemed to have shifted into a different focus.

'I think it's time to go, don't you?' Again his words were only for her, but there wasn't much of a question in them. They were a statement that didn't invite discussion.

Speechless, Zelda nodded. The sooner they got out of there the better, as far as she was concerned. She didn't know what was happening to her.

Conversation continued between Aram and the driver for most of the journey to Malatya, but between Aram and Zelda there was almost total silence. She found the atmosphere that had been created between them since the game in the café impossible. She couldn't wait to contact Mehmet. Then at last she could be free of this deeply disturbing stranger who seemed to be taking over her life.

CHAPTER FOUR

IT WAS well into the evening by the time they arrived in the town that was familiar to Zelda through her dealings with her carpet contact. Mehmet's family lived some distance away from Malatya in the mountainous area to the south, but he had a small shop in the town which was run by his eldest son, and which he used as a base for his larger operations.

Zelda's contact with him had originally been made by chance, but she now counted him as a friend as well as a colleague. In a personal context he was kind and helpful; in business he was vital to her, providing her with a reliable base in eastern Turkey, where she did much of her buying, and arranging for the transportation of about eighty per cent of her purchases by cheap means—usually contacts through friends of his. It sometimes resulted in vital stock getting held up for a few weeks on its way through Europe, which had unfortunate repercussions as far as their London sales were concerned, but nothing had been lost yet. Although both Mehmet and his associates had to make some money out of the arrangements, in their present financial straits the Magic Carpets Company had decided that it was a much cheaper method of transportation than investment in their own truck and driver, or paying to send the stuff by air.

So, as far as Zelda was concerned, it was very bad news when she could contact neither Mehmet nor his son at the shop, over which one or the other of them lived during the working days of the week.

'No luck with your friend?' Aram had enquired on his way through the foyer of the hotel in which, to her dismay, he had chosen to book in along with her on their arrival in Malatya. They hadn't discussed it, but she had assumed he would be staying somewhere else.

She hadn't told Mehmet precisely when she'd be delivering the new stock, but she'd let him know about her proposed trip to Syria, and expected him to be looking out for her. She'd never known him to be away before.

'He'll be in tomorrow,' she told her unwanted companion with a confidence she didn't feel.

The sooner she and Aram separated, the better. She still hadn't found out what he did for a living, but, gunrunner or not, it wasn't so much his occupation that bothered her now. For other reasons entirely, she couldn't wait to be out of his company. What had happened in the café had been more than just a game: Aram might have set it up only as a kind of revenge, but to her it had been a revelation. She was aware now of just how intensely she was attracted to him—and he knew it.

She was afraid of herself. Although she hadn't been involved with anyone for over a year—ever since she and Melanie had first had the idea of starting up the Magic Carpets Company, in fact—that last all too painful love-affair had left her very wary. She never seemed to be able to cope with her own disastrous ability to fall head over heels for the wrong man. It was something that had in the past happened very quickly, and as far as this disturbing stranger was concerned she'd had all the warning signals already. And never in her life had she met anyone with quite such a powerful effect on her as Aram Kalinsky had.

So, whoever he was, it was definitely time to say goodbye before what had actually proved to be quite a useful encounter turned into a totally destructive one.

'Aram, I want to thank you,' she said quickly. 'It was very kind of you to see me along all this way. I don't suppose we'll meet in the morning—I've got to get hold of Mehmet, and then I'm sure he'll be able to get me a lift to Istanbul. He's got dozens of useful contacts. I don't want to waste any more of your time.'

He was watching her in that disconcerting way of his all the way through her little speech.

'I've got plenty of time to waste—you're the one with the plane to catch,' he said slowly. 'What's the matter, Zelda—running away?' It was that very deep voice, with that kind of rough edge to it, which did exactly the same things to her as the nearness of his body.

She suppressed a shiver, and tried to look as though she didn't know what he was talking about. 'I just thought it would be much easier to work it this way, that's all.' She was going to babble, protest too much, and to lose this discussion if she didn't escape fast. The best way of getting the last word was to leave before he could say anything else. 'Running away? Of course I'm not. What would I be running away from?' Then she turned abruptly to do just that!

Too late. His hand was on her arm, and he forced her gently round to face him.

'Me?' he suggested, and held her eyes.

Her voice seemed to stick in her throat.

There was a loaded silence and then he said, 'Because if you are running away from me, you're not going to find it easy, my pretty little carpet dealer. For all sorts of reasons, I don't want you to disappear yet.'

'What—what sort of reasons?' she faltered, wondering if she was hearing him right, confused between the way he had paid her a compliment and the unnerving suspicion that he *was* up to some black market operations and wanted her for cover.

His look assessed her. 'Well, for one,' he said slowly, 'you're nice to kiss and I'd like to try it again some time when there isn't an amateur Arab removal service looking on.'

It wasn't what she'd expected. Involuntarily she took a step back, acutely conscious of his fingers still on her arm.

He laughed quietly and released her, noting quite openly the way she rubbed her skin as though his touch had left some mark, but he didn't comment on it. Instead, his words were matter-of-fact, and to the point.

'I'll give you a lift to your friend's shop tomorrow with the carpets. You don't want to be loading them in and out of a taxi. I've already made enquiries about hiring a car, and there'll be no problem. See you in the morning. Sleep well.'

'But——!'

But Aram knew the same tricks as she did. And it was he who got out before she could reply.

Unless she could leave the hotel before him in the morning, there would be no way of avoiding him. He was far too forceful. Maybe his interest in keeping her company *was* to do with cover for his doubtful 'business', but, after what had happened between them in the café earlier, and what he had just said to her, she could no longer doubt that that powerful attraction was mutual.

Well, there was *no way* she was going to get mixed up with someone like Aram no matter how attractive she found him, she told herself later, as she tossed on the narrow mattress that felt as though it had been made of jumbled bricks. And as for his 'sleep well', that must have been meant as the joke it was—she seemed to have been awake for hours! How could she be expected to sleep when every time she shut her eyes she got an image in her mind of Aram's face...that predatory aquiline nose, and piratical eye-patch...and then that tall, well-knit body that had such a disturbing effect on her own? Even thinking about him brought her out in goose-bumps... She would *have* to get up early.

'You're an emotional disaster area, Zel—I can't imagine how anyone with your talent for driving a hard bargain and such good business sense can be so hopeless when it comes to intimate relationships! You're entirely ruled by your feelings of the moment. Don't you ever stop to think what might happen *before* you get yourself involved with someone?'

She could hear Melanie's all too accurate criticism echoing in her head as she woke from an unusually troubled sleep... Sleep! She didn't think she'd been to sleep—what time was it, for heaven's sake?

The hands of her travelling-alarm pointed to half-past seven, and there was noise enough in the street to suggest that the entire population of Malatya was about its morning affairs. Why hadn't she woken up when her clock rang? Then she saw that the little button had been pushed down, and dimly, somewhere in the middle of all those confused dreams about herself and a tall, hawk-faced man with black hair, she remembered the shrilling of a bell that had seemed to be something to do with telephones at the time. She must have switched it off without even realising.

Washing and dressing with record speed, she debated the problem awaiting her downstairs. She didn't have much hope of escaping Aram now. She'd insisted that the hotel locked up her carpets overnight in a safe room, and had signed an impromptu receipt for them—that would mean a while before she could repossess them and pile them into a waiting taxi. All the more time for Aram to appear and start to interfere with her arrangements once more.

Slipping her assortment of rings on to slim fingers, she told herself—yet again—why it was imperative that she should spend no more time in the company of Aram Kalinsky. One: he must be up to no good, with all that so-called merchandise he had kept locked into the boot of the hired car, and hadn't let her get so much as a glimpse of since. What he had done with those boxes since his arrival in the hotel was a mystery—if he had checked them into the safe room, then he had done it when she wasn't around. Two: she didn't want to get involved with anyone who was into shady business deals—drugs, guns, maybe even smuggling alcohol into a Muslim country—it didn't matter what. Three: he might be a terrorist, which was far worse than any black marketeer. And four, most ridiculously disturbing of all: no matter how suspicious she might be about him as a character, she already found him physically far too attractive for her own peace of mind, and he'd made it clear he wasn't indifferent to her either. Four very good reasons indeed why she should get away as quickly as possible from a man who was still—despite everything that had happened—almost a total stranger to her.

The one lift wasn't working, and he was in the foyer when she got down to the bottom of the stairs, breathless from the speed of her descent.

She stared at him. The patch was gone—and with it, instantly, her more dramatic imaginings. He looked no more than a tall, dark and exceptionally handsome man. But, even at the distance she was standing from him, she could see the faint pinkish tinge in his newly revealed left eye.

'Oh!' The exclamation had a hint of disappointment about it that was purely involuntary. 'That's conjunctivitis!'

The dark brows lifted in surprise, and then Aram laughed. 'What were you hoping for—a rose-coloured glass eye I could pop in and out?'

She'd asked for that. The unguarded tone of her remark must have given away her lurid speculations, but before she could reply he went on, 'I was about to come up to see if you were still there—I was wondering if some local pasha hadn't stolen you away in the night to be the jewel of his harem...'

'Don't be ridiculous!' she said tartly, and then felt a bit guilty—it wasn't his fault she had jumped to some dramatic conclusions about that piratical patch; she could have asked. She was never at her best when she'd just got up.

'Get out of bed the wrong side?' he enquired, in just the tone that could contribute to a nicely weighed insult. But there was a gleam of humour in those disconcerting eyes.

'No.' She gave him a defiant glare, instantly on the defensive. She wasn't sure what there was to be defensive about, except that the new image was even more dangerously attractive than the old all of a sudden.

There was no dining-room attached to the little hotel, which furnished only the basics for the economy-minded traveller, but she knew where to get a good Continental breakfast at a café down the road. She was going to waste as long a time as possible over her yoghurt and coffee so that Mr Handsome, Sexy and most probably Dishonest Kalinsky would get fed up with waiting and go off on his own concerns. An innocent reason for the eye-patch didn't mean that he *wasn't* gun-running, she reminded herself sourly.

Ignoring him, she greeted the receptionist, and asked to use the phone. It would be worth trying to contact Mehmet now—he might even have a van to fetch the carpets.

There was still no answer from his shop, and that was unnerving. Even at this hour he was usually at work. She decided to leave it till later, and, without so much as a backward glance at her companion, she marched straight out of the hotel and down the road to Kemal's. The only way to deal with Kalinsky was to be firm with him—and herself.

She might have known he would follow her. And that he would sit opposite her at the same table. And that despite her hostile glare he would engage her in the kind of conversation which suggested that everything was settled between them, and that any objections she might have to travelling further with him were entirely irrelevant. She felt so uncomfortable in his presence that the only defence she could think of was to be rude to him.

'I have to pick up my own car in Kayseri,' he was saying. 'I've already arranged about leaving the hired one there. When did you say your flight left from Istanbul?'

'I didn't.'

'I thought you said something about three days?'

'I don't remember.' She bit off an enormous chunk of bread which would effectively prevent her from explaining further, and gazed pointedly out of the plate glass window of Kemal's which had the Turkish word for 'restaurant' written backwards across it. She knew she was behaving childishly, but blamed it on the way that Aram was unnerving her by scrutinising her from the other side of the table, and on his amusement.

She found that she needed to say something, so she chewed very fast. With what felt like half a loaf pushed into one cheek, she swallowed and announced, before her determination could fade, 'Thank you very much for your help yesterday, Ar—Mr Kalinsky, but I have quite a bit of business to see to today and it's better I don't take up any more of your time.'

She thought she had managed to sound quite cold and dismissive, given her handicap, but it didn't seem to have the slightest effect.

'You look like a hamster like that,' he pointed out, in friendly tones, his eyes on her. 'I had a pet hamster when I was a boy. My sister and I used to fight over whose turn it was to feed it.'

Zelda stared at him from under her page-boy fringe, and tried not to choke. It was difficult to imagine him with a sister, let alone a domestic pet. The absence of the brigand's eye-patch seemed to be signalling a change in more than just the physical impression he had made on her.

'I told you yesterday I wasn't going to let you get away so easily. What *are* your objections to a perfectly good lift to Istanbul?'

By the time she had safely swallowed the last of the bread, she'd thought better of all the more dramatic accusations she had been tempted to make, and settled for a few of her more reasonable objections.

'I don't know anything about you,' she said, less firmly than she had intended. 'I've got lots of valuable carpets with me—at least they're potentially valuable to anyone who knows how to sell them—and you're expecting me to travel across more than half Turkey with you. How do I know I can trust you?'

He gave her a long, considering look, and then he said, 'What's the worst thing that you think is likely to happen—murder? Rape? Theft? The car breaking down in the wilds of Anatolia?'

'All of them.'

'Come on—I'm being serious!' he protested, but that amused gleam still lurked there somewhere, and she had to admit to herself that, with the threat of that predatory eye-patch gone, he might even turn out to be the sort of person she could really get to like. 'You can't compare murder with a flat tyre, and if it's murder you're expecting then I have to disappoint you. I'm not the murderous type. You have to take my word for that. Besides, if there *is* anything I'd like to do to you, it's not along those lines.'

'You mean you might rape me instead?'

'It might cross my mind,' he said slowly, with a quirk of that well-shaped mouth, 'if you provoked me enough, but somehow I don't think it's going to come to that.'

So what did that mean exactly—that she wouldn't provoke him enough? Or that she would, but it wouldn't be rape because he believed she'd be only too willing?

The words were left deliberately ambiguous, and he went on, 'Anyway, I thought that was what your nearly black-belt in judo was all about. And as to theft—again there are no guarantees, but if, as you so forcefully pointed out yesterday, I don't know the first thing about carpets, how am I going to make a profit on them that would make stealing them worthwhile? That only leaves the breakdown in the wilds of Anatolia, and I can assure you we'll be keeping strictly to the main road.'

There were some terrible gaps in the argument, but it wasn't even worth her while to point them out. She wouldn't be travelling with him, and that was the end of the matter.

It didn't help that he waited patiently until she had finished every last drop, crumb and spoonful of her breakfast, and stood at the café door to let her go out first. Then, as she hung back to avoid brushing past him in the narrow doorway, he reached forward to run a finger down her nose in a light caress that rooted her to the spot. All the nerve-ends in her body came instantly and startlingly alive, and she was aware of every inch of the powerful masculine frame so close to her.

'You're an exceptionally pretty little carpet dealer, Miss Black Belt, Poker-Playing Ferrari Driver...'

That low, edgy voice had its effect on her too. But she was totally unprepared for what he was saying.

'... What you do to me you probably can't even guess at. But two things I'm going to promise you: with murder ruled out and breakdowns strictly unguaranteeable, I'm going to have that carpet of yours in the end... and——' that almost animal purr in his voice deepened '—I'm going to have *you*! There'll be no theft, and there certainly won't be any rape. So what do you say to that, Zelda Denton?'

For an endless moment, she stared up sat him. She didn't know what to say. Everything that she had only sensed between them yesterday seemed to have become a reality she wasn't ready for, and the relationship had suddenly taken a giant step along just the path she'd been trying to avoid.

Her heart was racing, and she was finding it difficult to breathe evenly, but lifted her chin in defiance. 'I say you're out of your mind, Aram Kalinsky, because I'm not going to Istanbul with you, or anywhere else, and

we're saying goodbye *now* here in this street at precisely——' she glanced pointedly at her watch '—twenty-
five minutes to nine this morning!'

So how was it, she asked herself precisely one hour later,
that she now found herself sitting beside him in the third
vehicle he had hired during their brief acquaintance, on
her way to Konya, famed city of the Whirling Dervishes?

In her own defence, she could claim that it had a lot
to do with the fact that Mehmet had gone—with his
son—to a family wedding in the mountains, and that
Zelda herself didn't possess a key to the shop, and that
none of the neighbours had been entrusted with one.
Aram's Turkish had, she was forced to admit, been in-
valuable in establishing all the relevant facts—even to
the discovery that Mehmet had said he was leaving a key
with a cousin, though when the cousin was found it
transpired that he had forgotten.

Zelda knew that without taking undue pride in it she
could call herself efficient when it came to organising
her dealing, but she couldn't hold a candle to Aram.
Without appearing to hurry in the least, he had sorted
his way through a dozen different versions of the Mehmet
saga, visited four different locations in search of the key,
interviewed innumerable relatives and friends, and still
had time to drink a glass of tea with the absent dealer's
next-door neighbour. Following breathless in his wake,
she had been forced into a grudging admiration of his
skill—perhaps that was why she hadn't objected further
when it came to accepting the long-debated lift.

Having to take the carpets with her was a serious
drawback. On her own, she would probably have had
to hire a car as a last resort, and that would have reduced her profits. With the business running on a shoe-
string, they really couldn't afford any extra expenses. To
give him his due, Aram had been prepared to discuss
alternatives with her, but it very quickly became clear
that there weren't any. The only solution was to go with

him—all the way to Istanbul, unless something miraculous happened on the way. Once she got there, she wasn't sure what she would do with her stock, but she would meet that problem when she came to it.

Her grave doubts about her companion prompted her to consult a road map, which Aram produced on demand without comment. But she was unnerved by the fact that while she studied the map, he studied her... Suspiciously, she assessed the route: given that he had to pick up his own car at Kayseri and had business in Konya—and she only had his word for that—the journey he proposed was not an unreasonable one. But she was glad she had given him an early deadline for her flight from Istanbul: it was a way of insuring against any avoidable delays.

Once on the road, they didn't speak much, even to remark on passing traffic, which included from time to time men with donkeys or mules beside the road, or headscarfed women, their skirts hitched up to show voluminous Turkish trousers, making their way between villages with animals or children. Familiar sights to Zelda, they left her free to follow her own thoughts. Should she leave Aram at Kayseri? If she didn't, where exactly would they find themselves that night...?

Kayseri was a fair-sized, unremarkable town that Zelda had been in before, and she wasn't sorry when Aram showed no signs of lingering. His car, a large Ford estate, was being looked after by a friend whose house they visited briefly.

'Why didn't you take this to Syria?' she demanded when she saw it. It looked much better than anything he had hired, and was ideally suited to transporting 'merchandise'—whatever he had meant by that; she still hadn't discovered.

He gave her a wry grin. 'It broke down. Murat was getting it mended for me.' It was an admission that amused her, in the light of their first disastrous driving experience.

'Going too fast?' she enquired sweetly, and, noting the quick frown, wasn't surprised when he refrained from comment. In some of his moods, he was surprisingly easy to offend.

She didn't know whether it was that remark that caused him to speed up on the next part of their journey, but the road was not a fast one and the skilful but nerve-racking way he overtook slower vehicles eventually scared her so much she demanded that he pull over to the side.

'What's the matter—don't you feel well?' he asked with a glance of concern as they scudded to a halt that raised a thick cloud of dust over a passing flock of goats. She was already opening the door.

'Take my stuff out of the back right *now*!' she demanded. 'I'm not going one more *inch* of this road with you! What are you trying to do—kill us? I'm waiting right here for a civilised lorry driver, even if it takes all night!'

She stormed round to the back of the car, and then found that he'd locked it. He didn't get out, and she was at his side in seconds, her hand stretched through the open side-window.

'Give me the keys!'

'And if I refuse?' He eyed her speculatively.

'I'm not getting back in there unless you let me drive.'

'Have you got your licence?'

'Yes,' she said defiantly. 'And my insurance!'

'I could drive off with all your carpets and leave you...'

She glared at him, hating him suddenly and passionately with every fibre in her body. He was every bit the brigand he had first looked! His milder moments were just a ploy to deceive her, and he had consciously exploited that latent attraction between them to keep her with him. 'Like hell you will! I'll have the police after you before you can get halfway to Konya!'

She glared at him, expecting an answering hostility in him, but this time he was grinning. Probably enjoying the way he had riled her, she thought furiously. How

childish! Suddenly he took the keys from the ignition
and put them into her hand.

'All right,' he said. 'You choose. Unload your stuff,
or drive the car. It doesn't matter to me.'

She continued to glare at him, undecided. It would be
very, very inconvenient to have to pile everything on to
the road... And he knew it.

With a word, she pulled open the door and waited for
him to get out.

'I'll drive,' she said, and bit her lip to prevent herself
adding a few gratuitous insults.

Aram didn't get out, merely shifting his long legs
across the gear-stick and levering himself into the passenger seat.

It didn't help that she couldn't get the car into first
gear without a struggle, nor that, in the resulting stress,
she forgot to look in her mirror before she pulled out
into the road. The oppressive silence of his forbearance,
as a heavy truck roared by within inches of them, was
worse than if he'd shouted at her.

It wasn't long before he told her to turn off the road
to her right.

'We won't make Konya tonight,' he explained. 'It's
over a hundred and fifty miles yet, and we're not on a
three-lane motorway, more's the pity.'

'I'd never have guessed from the way you drive,' she
retorted, but was relieved when he chose to ignore it.
She'd come to the conclusion that she wasn't good at
predicting his reactions.

'We'll stop at Akseray, which is about halfway,' he
said, after a brief silence. 'I want to see someone who
makes carpets in one of the villages round here.'

'What do you want to see a carpet dealer for?' she
asked quickly, torn between two possible explanations—
one, that he was deliberately delaying the journey, and
two, less likely, that he might be doing it for her... Despite her suspicions of him, a flattering spark of hope

told her that, after what he had said that morning about being attracted to her, the second was just possible. But the spark was instantly quenched.

'I'm collecting souvenirs,' he said shortly. And then, 'Ever been in this area before?'

She knew well the fascinating stone valley of Göreme, full of cave dwellings and beautifully painted rock churches that was the tourist high-spot of the whole area, and merely nodded, concentrating on driving. Now they were off the main highway, the village roads were narrow and could be tricky. You never knew when you might meet a donkey with heavily laden panniers, or a flock of goats wandering in the road.

'I've travelled all over Turkey,' she said after a while. 'What about you?'

'The same. I love this part of the world—especially the mountains. And I love the village people and their way of life.' It was the first time he had volunteered information with such a genuine enthusiasm, and she didn't want to waste this more communicative mood.

'Do you speak fluent Turkish? It sounds like it. Thanks for helping me sort out the problems over Mehmet's absence this morning, by the way.'

She caught his eye, and he gave a fleeting smile. 'My pleasure. I'm glad the Turkish sounded convincing—but I have to confess it's pretty ungrammatical.'

'English, Arabic, Turkish—you're quite a linguist,' she commented, a very real admiration warming the husky tones of her voice.

'My sister and I were brought up in a multi-lingual household,' he explained. 'We hadn't much choice. We spoke Polish or French at home, depending on who was there, and English at school. Then, some years ago, I went to live in Paris for a bit. And I travel a lot—I suppose that accounts for it.'

'So how do you know about this carpet dealer?' she asked after another pause for navigation.

'Through a friend—turn left here—he's supposed to have some quite interesting stuff. Not that I'd know, of course.' There was a heavy irony in that last remark, and he followed it up with, 'That's why I've brought an expert with me...'

'Well, I *am* an expert!' she replied, stung. 'Knowing good carpets from bad is how I make my living.' Perhaps I'll get him to buy some awful old rubbish just for revenge! she thought. The idea was appealing, and she dwelt on it.

It took them ages to find the dealer he was looking for, and there were several interviews with villagers before Aram located the house, cut into a rock face that formed three walls of the dwelling. The light had already begun to fade outside, and the room into which they were taken was so gloomy it was difficult to see the quality of any of the wares.

Aram insisted on taking some of the small woven kilims outside, but in the event Zelda had no chance to play her trick on him. The craftsmanship was obviously poor and the dyes crude, and when she tried suggesting with feigned enthusiasm that one of them could be quite attractive, he merely said bluntly, 'No, it couldn't—it's rubbish.' And then gave her a curious look.

Her lips curved in amusement. 'So you do know a little about carpets after all?'

'I know what I like,' he said, with one of those sudden flashing smiles in answer to hers.

But while she hadn't been able to interpret everything she'd read in those light green eyes, the tone in which he had spoken ran a little shiver through her—he'd made it obvious that it wasn't just carpets he was talking about.

She never knew where she was with him—one moment they were quarrelling, and the next he was paying her backhanded compliments. The arguments she had been determined to win, she seemed to have lost, and then, when she least expected it, he gave in to her. She hadn't forgotten his boast that morning—or had it been a threat?—that he'd have the Turkish carpet, *and her*. He'd openly admitted he found her physically attractive, but surely that didn't account for his unpredictable changes of mood . . . or was it he who found her unpredictable?

Well, if it was all just some sort of game, she was determined it wasn't one he was going to win.

CHAPTER FIVE

THEY lost their way after that.

Zelda wasn't sure whose fault it was—she supposed she should have been mapping their route in her mind as she was following Aram's directions, but, with the varied instructions given to them by the villagers, she no longer had any idea where they were. Aram claimed to, until they found themselves in a valley they hadn't seen before. There were high caves to one side and a grove of alder trees to the other, but not a sign of a habitable dwelling nor a single villager. Again the suspicion crossed her mind that he had decided to leave the main highway for a reason that had little to do with carpets, and she remembered his joke about a breakdown in the wilds...and about theft...and about rape. But she had no time to weigh up the situation.

It had been growing rapidly darker for some time, the blackening clouds obscuring the last of the evening sunshine. She had switched on the car's headlights to cope with the worsening visibility, but all of a sudden two thigns happened: the cloudburst, that had been threatening since they had headed towards Göreme, fell on them with just the briefest warning rattle of drops before the windscreen was a running waterfall—and then both headlights failed.

'Don't stop just here!' Aram said curtly. 'This dried-up valley will act as a watercourse—get the car on to higher ground.'

'But I can't see where I'm going,' she protested. 'I might drive it into a tree!'

'For heaven's sake!' He sounded suddenly exasperated. 'There's a higher strip running along to your right—*no!* Not like that!'

79

She had let up the clutch too quickly, and as the wheels spun uselessly under the car he reached right across her and turned off the ignition. There was something so unnerving about his sudden blast of anger, directed at her, that she found herself shaking.

'Quickly—get out.'

'In that downpour? You must be joking!' But even her protest had lost its usual self-assurance.

He didn't wait to argue, but was out of his own door and round her side before she had had time to think. There was no ceremony about the way he grasped one arm, his fingers biting into her flesh as he hauled her out to leave her standing in the pouring rain, while he restarted the car.

The cold torrent poured down her face and hair, running down her neck and soaking her clothes, her canvas shoes quickly becoming sodden in the little stream that was already beginning to flow across the stones and hard-packed earth of the valley floor. But she was too humiliated and uncomfortable to admit that Aram had been right to move the car immediately—the gulley in which she was standing would soon become a muddy sea.

Clasping her arms across her chest, she squinted through the freezing rain to the higher ground where the Ford was now parked. The sounds of its engine ceased abruptly, and there was only the noise of the rain. The driver's door opened.

'Zelda, come here you little idiot, before you catch your death of cold!' His voice didn't sound in the least sympathetic—in fact he still sounded furious. As if it were her fault that the weather had suddenly decided to turn nasty!

She ran to the car, shivering, clothes clinging to her, but as she tried to get in the passenger side, he stopped her.

'Wait—take those things off first or you'll be sitting in a wet seat all the way to Istanbul.'

'What?' Even the discomfort of the rain became suddenly irrelevant.

'Come on—this isn't the time for false modesty. Take off your trousers and your sweatshirt. Have you got a towel in your bag?'

'Yes, but I'm not stripping in front of you!'

'You've got underwear on, haven't you? Hurry up. The rain's getting into the car.'

In furious embarrassment, she pulled down the fashionably loose cotton pants that were now clinging to her legs, but when she dropped them on the seat, he tossed them into the back of the car, on top of the pile of carpets. The rain was still pouring down, and her sweatshirt was sticking to her now as though it had been glued on.

'Come on!' he said again, with an impatience that gave an intimidating edge to those gruff tones. 'Take that thing off—I'm not waiting all night.'

She could feel every exposed inch of her skin—and a great many that weren't yet on view—flushing scarlet.

'I can't,' she said in a strangled voice. 'I haven't got anything on underneath.'

'Oh, for heaven's sake—do you think it's the first time I've seen a girl half naked?'

Reluctantly, she stripped off the sodden shirt, holding it in front of her until she could take the towel from his outstretched hand, and ducked into the car.

'Take your shoes off. You'll be warmer that way.' She had wrapped the towel round her with a struggle, not helped by the fact that he was watching every movement, and now she bent to remove her espadrilles and toss them into the back with the shirt.

'I wouldn't have got so wet if you hadn't driven off like that!' she accused, but she was acutely conscious of the fact that she *was* half naked, and couldn't look him in the eye.

'You wouldn't have got so wet if you hadn't stopped to argue with me,' he pointed out unsympathetically.

'How do you think I feel about the prospect of driving all the way to Akseray like this?' she demanded.

'You've got more clothes, haven't you? But you needn't worry—we're not going anywhere until it gets light.'

'What do you mean?'

'We can't drive without headlights, and there's no way I'm getting out in this downpour to fiddle about with the electrics. It might just be faulty wiring, but if both bulbs have gone there's not much I can do about it until tomorrow. We're staying here.'

Zelda had long been acquainted with the phrase about hearts sinking, but she had never supposed it was literally true until now—she felt hers very definitely drop, right the way down to her cold bare toes.

'Oh,' she said, weakly. It was useless to argue. Especially when she couldn't even stop shivering.

There was a silence, until he said, 'Zelda...?' She turned towards him, clutching the towel to her protectively, and preparing for further hostilities.

He was looking at her in a way she couldn't quite interpret—it wasn't exactly exasperation, but neither was it neutrally friendly. Their eyes met, hers full of doubt, and then incredibly his changed and she was astonished this time by what she could read in them—laughter.

She began to laugh just when he did, and she scarcely noticed as his arm slipped round her bare shoulders, and he pulled her close, hugging her against him.

'I've met some women in my time, but you're the most incredible, Zelda Denton,' he said in her ear. 'And for reasons that you know nothing about—as well as the obvious ones—you're driving me crazy...' His voice was low and unsteady, with laughter, and with something else... And that must have been when everything suddenly changed.

There was a second's hesitation, and then she was aware of his lips on the side of her face, tracing a swift line from her ear to her chin until she knew he was going to kiss her mouth and she was longing for it—she turned her face up to his without a thought, twining her arms round his neck and pressing closer.

Instantly he pulled her towards him so that she was almost lying against him, stretched out right across her own seat—a few inches more and she'd have been in his lap. His mouth touched the side of hers, and then, tantalisingly, his tongue slid along between her lips to part them, his own softly persuasive, until with a little sigh she let him do what he wanted.

And she wanted it too—somehow it had seemed inevitable since those first extraordinary moments in the Syrian desert when he had lifted her from a truck piled high with rickety furniture. The powerful reactions he had awoken in her then blazed up anew as his mouth moved expertly on hers, and it was as though he were pouring liquid fire down her veins so that her limbs, still cold from the rain, were filled with some magical quicksilver running through her until she was no longer aware of anything but the ache of a very explicit need that was beginning to overpower her. With no conscious thought of what she was doing and no heed of the consequences, she responded to the skilful persuasion, darting her tongue between his lips, provoking him into a new exploration that sent that dizzying lightning through her once more as her body registered his response. Never in her whole life had she felt sensations so overwhelming, and it both terrified and excited her so that she was quickly oblivious of everything except the sensual demands of her body.

On some instinctive level, she must have known that he could do this to her from their very first encounter.

It was he who pulled back first, and she could feel his rapid uneven breathing against her. He didn't say anything, but brushed the hair back from her face with gentle repeated strokes and then ran his fingers across her bare shoulder and down her arm, gathering her towards him again to hold her against him. It was then she realised that he hadn't made any attempt to caress her more intimately; she was practically naked, wearing only a precariously hitched bathtowel and a pair of scanty briefs and he'd hardly even touched her—and she'd been almost ready to give herself to him there and then! Shame flooded through her, as she was forced to acknowledge to herself that, although he had made the first move, it had been she who was leading, not he...

More humiliated than she had ever felt in her life, she pushed herself out of his arms.

He didn't attempt to hold her, and made no move to entice her back, and she didn't know how to look at him again after that. He had been amusing himself—he had even told her yesterday that he would kiss her again, when there was no Arab to look on. It was all part of that game, just like the bidding for the carpet. But she, like a fool, had forgotten all her resolutions and had virtually offered herself to him. It was too painful to speculate on what he must think of her.

Turning away from him to hide her confusion, she reached back to find her holdall, dragging out her jeans and the first thick sweater she could lay her hands on, pulling the latter over her head before she removed the covering towel.

The jeans were not so easy to manage, but she wriggled into them, trying to ignore the amused grin she knew Aram was giving her. Then, unexpectedly, he reached out to caress the side of her face in one smooth gesture. 'What's the matter? Don't tell me you're an outraged virgin, because I won't believe it.'

'I wasn't going to tell you anything of the kind.' Her reply was awkwardly defensive because after that shameful and undeniable proof of just how overwhelmingly attractive she found him, she didn't really know what to say.

'Of what kind?' he pursed relentlessly. 'Outrage or virginity?'

'Both—neither. Though I don't see it's any of your business!'

'It might be if the outrage was on behalf of some boy-friend back home...'

'I haven't got a boyfriend back home!' And instantly she regretted that admission—a mythical boyfriend in England, a six-foot-two rugger fanatic for preference—might act as a useful deterrent. But underneath she still had to admit that it wasn't his desires she'd had to control, but her own, and no mythical English rugger player was going to be able to cope with those...

She could feel him looking at her. 'So the quick change of clothes indicates a change of mood?' He didn't sound annoyed—only unaccountably pleased about something.

She couldn't think of an uncompromising answer so she pretended to ignore him, and then sat in an uncomfortable silence listening to the rain until he switched on the ignition again to turn on the car radio. Even if he had been stalling a bit on the journey, she told herself, he couldn't have planned on *everything* that had just happened.

How long they sat there listening to the rain drumming on the roof and the strange wailing cadences of Turkish pop singers she never knew, but it was dark when he said, 'We can stay here until morning but we'd be much more comfortable up in those caves. It'll get very cold down here on the valley floor and we can't run the engine all night.'

Still caught up in the aftermath of the confusion of feelings he had caused in her, for once she wasn't prepared to argue.

If he thought it was a better idea to spend the night in the caves, so be it. It was his decision, and, provided that he didn't leave her alone up there, she would go along with it. She couldn't afford another quarrel if it was going to end the way the last one just had. But at least she wouldn't have to sit with him all night with no more than twelve inches of space between them.

On his instructions, they took an armful each of the rugs from the car—her Turkish favourite among them. She wasn't prepared to leave it to be stolen by any passing opportunist before morning. It was still raining—only lightly now—but the wet ground was slippery underfoot and what would have been an easy approach in daylight became an undignified scramble in Aram's wake.

She liked the idea less and less as they approached the dark caverns halfway up the shadowy rock face—in daylight they had looked interesting but innocuous. Now they seemed to harbour an unknown threat.

'Are you sure we'll be safe here?' she asked once, a slight tremor in her voice betraying her unspoken fears. The familiar laugh was reassuring.

'Perfectly—unless you're afraid of bats?'

She was. But she wasn't going to admit it.

When they eventually reached a level access to one of the caves, his flashlight showed them a wide, dry room with a dusty rock floor, one wall open to the night. There were a couple of dark doorways cut out of the rock each side leading further into the complex of man-made caverns, which had once been the dwellings of an early Christian community.

Zelda shivered; she wished now she had stayed in the car, but she didn't want to provoke any comment. She still felt far too embarrassed about what had just happened between them. She was convinced she had made a monumental fool of herself, and she needed time to find some sort of defence against his particular brand of sarcasm.

They found that they were not the only ones to have had the idea of taking shelter there—there was a pile of old wood by one wall and the charred remains of a fire in the centre of the room. The rain was still falling beyond the mouth of the cave, and she watched while Aram squatted down to set an experimental match to some of the branches. The wood proved to be dry, and some of the smaller twigs caught quickly. Zelda looked on helplessly, unwilling to stay too close to him in case he should misinterpret it, and nervous of the dark shadows that leapt in the flickering glow that was beginning to light their curious dwelling.

'I'm not sleeping out in the middle,' she announced at last, 'even if it is nearer the fire. I'd like to know there's at least one solid wall behind me. And, anyway, it looks as though that wood isn't going to last very long.'

She would have been happier in a corner—with two walls rather than one to protect her—but the dark doorways were much too close to each of the corners on the far wall of the room, and the fourth wall was missing.

The glow of the dying branches seemed very feeble, and very far away, when she finally selected her portion of wall to sleep against. Not too close to the open side of the room, and as far as she could get from the doorways. She spread one of her rugs on the floor—she couldn't tell which one it was in the dark, but hoped it was one of the cheapest—and then heaped up her bags and the rest of her rugs on top of it.

Wrapping the stiff canvas and wool round her wasn't easy, and she huddled against the wall, trying to make herself as small as possible. The night air was very chilly, but she was aware that the rain had stopped—the dark clouds were breaking up, and she could see stars.

Aram had a couple of kilims, and she wondered about asking him if she could do a swap—one of her carpets in exchange for a softer warmer rug for the night. But something told her he would inevitably take advantage of the situation. She could just make out where he was settling his own bedding, close to the fire, and then the noises of shuffling and rearrangement ceased. All of a sudden it was horribly silent.

'This is an awful cave!' she complained in a half-whisper, trying to keep the nervousness out of her voice when she couldn't bear the silence any longer—then gave an unguarded squeak as something dark seemed to brush past her swiftly towards the night outside, and the stars that now filled the missing wall like a giant television screen.

Aram's reply sounded rather too distant, and not as encouraging as she would have liked.

'For such an independent business lady who's not afraid of bats, you've got some unexpected weak spots!' And then, after a pause, 'What would you do if you were on your own?'

'I wouldn't be in this mess if I were on my own!' she hissed back, unwilling to raise her voice in that vast silence. 'I'd be in a nice little cheap hotel somewhere, sleeping in a bed with sheets, not rolled up in a lot of musty carpets—eek!'

'What's the matter?' He didn't sound in the least sympathetic, only lazily amused.

'It's all very well for you to find it funny but something touched me, I'm sure of it!' Her heart seemed to be galloping with fright, and her eyes were wide in the darkness—not that she could see anything. That was half the trouble. 'Are there rats here?'

'How do I know? Just shut up for a while, there's a good girl. I want to get some sleep even if you don't.'

'But how can I sleep when all I can think of is horrible huge black rats with nasty yellow teeth swarming all over me in the night? They—they might have rabies . . . or the plague! Can you still catch the plague?' Turning her fears into a joke was a game she used to play at night with Dominic when they were children—only in the present circumstances it was making them worse, not better. She had almost convinced herself now that she could see something moving across the floor. A cold cramped night in the car would have been infinitely preferable to this!

She could hear Aram shifting his position.

'Why not give that colourful imagination of yours a rest?' he suggested, his voice heavy with the usual sarcasm.

She was silenced for a few moments by his tone, until she thought of a new danger.

'Are there snakes in these caves?'

He gave a theatrical sigh. 'Zelda, *please*! If you're scared come and sleep over here but for heaven's sake stop talking.'

'No. I mean I'm all right over here. Thank you.' It mightn't be just rats she was fighting off if she gave in to her fears and joined him by the fire. In fact, there probably weren't any rats at all—and she'd end up fighting herself as well as him if he touched her.

He gave a contemptuous snort, turned over restlessly again, and was quiet.

Time ticked away endlessly in the silence that followed. She found herself beginning to imagine sounds once more . . . or was she? Somewhere behind her in the darkness there were those huge black doorways—who knew what might come through them? Maybe it wasn't just rats who lived in these ancient caves. She'd heard plenty of stories about Turkish bandits who robbed tourists . . . and they mightn't be satisfied with money or her passport . . .

'Aram!' she whispered urgently. 'Are you awake?'

'Of course I'm awake. It's hardly three minutes since you were wittering on about snakes.'

'Switch on the torch!'

He groaned. 'Go to sleep.'

'I can't. Switch it on, please! I want to see where you are. The fire's gone out.'

He gave another groan, there were sounds of shuffling and then the rasp of a match being struck, and at last a sharp spurt of flame. It was a tiny light in all that blackness. It showed her his cupping hands, and highlighted those familiar aquiline features, before its feeble glow was lost in the huge darkness.

'Where's the torch?' she demanded shakily.

'Somewhere under the rugs—ow!'

She ignored the inventive and heartfelt curse that followed.

'Hold it steady—I'm coming over!' He might read it as an invitation to carry on where they had left off earlier in the car, but she would just have to take that risk. Better fight off someone she did know, than someone she didn't.

Gathering her bundles as best she could into the centre of the carpet she'd used to lie on, she crawled across to that welcome little flame, dragging everything behind her. The cave floor was uneven and hurt her knees, but it was preferable to tripping over every few steps.

He found another match while she re-sorted her impromptu bedding, more by touch than anything else. She thought better of asking him for one of the kilims. She'd have to admit she was cold, and that would give him an opening for the inevitable sort of banter. She didn't want him to think her capitulation was in any way a come-on, but at the same time she knew she'd be too terrified to sleep all night if she couldn't reassure herself of his presence. She settled for a gap of about two feet between them as a compromise.

'Get a move on,' he said impatiently. 'I'm not burning my fingers to charcoal sticks just so you can measure the distance between us down to the nearest inch. Do you really think ungovernable lust can be controlled by tape-measures?'

'I'm not measuring!' she protested crossly. 'I just don't want you to think...' Then she paused, stuck for the right words.

'To think what?' he demanded softly.

'Oh, all right, then—to think this is any sort of invitation, that's all! If it weren't for the rats, I'd probably be sleeping in another room!'

'But there aren't any rats.' That low, rough-edged voice was distinctly amused.

'Now he tells me! You know perfectly well what I mean, Aram Kalinsky.'

Then there was silence.

She still felt chilly, and she still wasn't convinced about absolute safety from rats—or any other unspecified threat from these ancient caves in the night. In fact, she didn't feel much safer than before.

She was tired, her very bones seemed to ache, but try as she might she couldn't keep her imagination under control. Just as she would begin to drift off in a doze, horrible images would begin to take over. She found herself wondering in the end if it really was Aram lying next to her—he was so still she couldn't be sure he was there. It seemed that every old horror film she'd ever seen was now coming back to haunt her.

She held her breath, listening for sounds that the man next to her was breathing, but she could hear nothing. He couldn't be asleep. People always breathed heavily when they were asleep. Why didn't he move? Surely he couldn't lie there like that for so long? Maybe he was dead... Don't be ridiculous, she told herself sharply. But instantly her imagination took over again—what if it wasn't Aram lying there—what if it was someone—some*thing*——?

'Aram!'

The undercurrent of panic in the low, urgent whisper gave her away.

'You really are a little fraidy cat, aren't you?' She heard the low, reassuring drawl.

There was again the sound of movement, and unexpectedly she felt herself being jerked sideways, rugs and all—he had caught hold of the carpet she was lying on and pulled it sharply towards him.

'Come here.'

And before she could even think to protest, he had shifted towards her, slipping two strong arms round her and drawing her against him.

'Don't get uptight again,' he said softly. 'I've got no intention of raping you. This is just to take your childish mind off the rats, and then we might both get some sleep...' Then, before she could say anything, his mouth was on hers.

But there was nothing aggressive, or threatening about the feel of him. She tensed to resist, intending to push him away and turn her head aside if she could, but before there was time to analyse what was happening she found herself relaxing back on to the carpet under him, pulling him closer, and then slipping her arms round his neck.

She could feel the abrasive texture of his unshaven chin and cheek against the sensitive skin of her face, and the strong muscular arms under her shoulders and back. A warm comfortable feeling began to uncurl in the pit of her stomach as, enjoying her release from her earlier fears, she shifted a little under him, pressing even closer. Perhaps this was going to prove a bad idea, but just at the moment she didn't care.

Instantly he responded, deepening the kiss, one arm sliding out from under her so that he could caress her, his hand tracing the fullness of her breast and then slipping down her side, over the curve of her waist and hip while his tongue explored her mouth.

The warm feeling inside her began to spread, sending little prickles of anticipation through her. It was all pleasantly languorous after her recent fears, with none of that electric urgency that seemed to have sparked through them both in the car. She slipped her fingers up through his hair, idly returning his caresses, deliberately banishing the knowledge that soon she was going to have to put a stop to this...

But when his hand moved to the zip of her jeans, she caught his wrist quickly, and then turned her head to break off the kiss, gasping a little. She was beginning to respond far more than she had imagined she would, but her reasons for not wanting it to go any further hadn't changed—she might find him overwhelmingly attractive, but he was still too much of an unknown quantity to get deeply involved with. And it would be deeply involved: there were no half-measures where she was concerned.

'No, Aram,' she said shakily.

She felt him release the zip, but his hand slipped down between her thighs, while he featherd the side of her face with tiny kisses. She reacted instantly to the touch of his hand, twisting away.

'Don't!' she protested a little desperately. 'You said no rape!'

'But it wouldn't be rape,' he murmured, his tongue finding the delicate whorls of her ear, and gently exploring. Then he broke off what he was doing to look down at her in the darkness. 'Would it?'

It was far too dark to read his expression, but she could see the glimmer of his eyes. Her skin felt cold now, where he'd licked it, and she hadn't really wanted him to stop.

'It would if you go on,' she said in half-hearted protest. 'Please don't.'

But her whole body was rapidly taking fire, and she was fighting herself as well as him, just as she had known she would be. All the weird fantasies of the dark cave had been banished completely—this was reality, insistent, demanding. If she let herself give in to her feelings now, that strong attraction between them from the very beginning would very quickly overwhelm them both.

Aram had propped himself on his elbows to look down at her. Now he took a deep breath and she could feel his rib-cage expanding against her own. He shifted his weight a little, his hips covering hers more closely so that she couldn't any longer doubt his arousal.

He let out a long, careful sigh. 'Oh...Zelda—you don't know what you're asking!' He kissed the tip of her nose, and then, as though he couldn't help himself, the side of her mouth, going on to tease at the provocative fullness of her underlip. 'You know, you're the sexiest little thing I've discovered in years... Why won't you? I promise it'd be good.'

Good sex—yes, she was sure it would be. There were enough of the vital sparks between them to ensure a truly explosive encounter. But that was all he was interested in, and that was why she didn't want it. What was there between them but a basic animal attraction, that this disturbing and strangely romantic setting could persuade her might be the beginning of something more for both of them? But the dull little voice of common sense told her that while the desire he had evoked still coursed through her she could be persuaded to anything.

He was reluctant to let her go. Perhaps, knowing where the real battle was going on, he was unwilling to give up his advantage. 'You fascinate me,' he said softly. 'Did you know that? Sometimes you almost remind me of a child in the direct way you react to things, but you're so independent—the street-wise little gamine. You know what you want.'

'Don't you?' The tone of his last remark puzzled her.

'I thought I did. Now I'm not so sure... You're very lovely, Zelda...'

There was something in his voice—some kind of suppressed emotion—that made his words sound more than just an unlikely compliment to gain his own ends, and she was tempted to let herself be persuaded by it. But he had shifted his weight again as he spoke to draw one finger gently down the side of her cheek, the initial movement thrusting his hips provocatively against hers so that she knew if she didn't stop him they would both be lost.

'I'm not at all lovely!' she said with an uneven laugh, trying to defuse some of the intensity between them. 'I'm not very clean, my hair needs washing, and it's only because you can't see me in the dark that you're saying things like that... You said you were going to take my mind off the rats——' she was trying to make it sound like a joke, even though she was sure he could feel her heart hammering against her ribs '—and you have. Very effectively... but I don't want this to go any further—please, Aram...'

If he decided to take her, there was nothing she could do to stop him. He was far too strong for her. And she wouldn't be able to claim it was rape—her mind might tell her it was foolish, but her body still wanted it. She wondered if she had at last come to the moment when she was going to discover the extent of that unscrupulousness she had sensed in him from the beginning—that hidden something, like a kind of power he kept in reserve.

She didn't actively resist him. It would have been stupid, and struggling might only have made things worse—he could even be the kind of man who liked his women fighting.

They lay like that for what was to her an age of indecision, and then finally some of the tension seemed to leave him. Without a word, he kissed her cheek in the darkness, and rolled away from her.

There was a long silence. She didn't know if she should say something or not. Perhaps he was angry? She had let him start this, and he could be forgiven for thinking of her as a tease. He had told her she knew what she wanted, but it couldn't apply to what had just happened between them—she had given very contradictory signals.

'Aram...?' Her tentative whisper was met with a forbidding silence.

'I'm sorry—after what happened in the car I shouldn't have let you...' Her voice trailed away. It was difficult to find the right words.

'OK,' he said, after a nerve-racking pause. From that, she couldn't tell whether he was angry or not. And then, to her relief, there was an unmistakable hint of humour in his voice, when he said, 'I should have left you to the rats.'

Later that night, only half awake, she found herself lying close against Aram's back, her body following the long contours of his. Her arm was round him, tucked under his, and he was holding her hand. He seemed to be asleep, breathing evenly and deeply, and her cheek was resting against his shoulder. She had no idea how she'd ended up like that but, asleep, he could be no threat to her, and that strong male presence so close kept the darkness at bay too.

She smiled, snuggling instinctively closer, and drifted into sleep again.

CHAPTER SIX

ZELDA woke because it was cold. There was a chilly grey light in the cave, and she found herself staring up at the high roughly chiselled ceiling, and wondering where she was. Then she turned to the man she had virtually shared a bed with last night, and found his place empty, the rugs still in a tumbled heap beside her.

She sat up quickly. 'Aram?'

He was sitting at the open edge of the cave, arms round knees, and a kilim draped over his shoulders. The missing wall was like a giant window, and she could see trees and a line of hills all shrouded in grey mist.

'I thought you'd never wake up,' he complained in heartfelt tones, stretching powerful arms out in front of him, and yawning. She heard his muscles crack. 'There's nothing to eat until we find our way out of this valley.'

Zelda's nose was cold, and her face felt stiff. 'It's freezing!' she moaned. 'I don't know which is worse— refrigeration or starvation.'

'It's a hell of a lot warmer in here than down in that fog. Come on, get up. The sooner we're on our way the better. And *I'm* driving this time.'

In the daylight, the route she had missed last night wasn't so difficult to find. They passed through a tiny hamlet, some of the ancient rock dwellings still inhabited by twentieth-century villagers whose ways hadn't changed so much from those of earlier occupants. Aram stopped the car and they got out, making for the village water trough, its sides spilling over with fresh, clean hill water.

A woman with a mule, its panniers piled high with vegetables, smiled at them and exchanged a few words with Aram in Turkish. She gave Zelda a large chunk of bread—a typical gesture of friendliness in the villages. When she had gone, Zelda tore the small loaf in half, although sorely tempted to eat the whole thing herself. Then she watched, chewing her share slowly and trying to make it last, while Aram stripped to the waist to wash in the icy water.

There was no one around, but she didn't feel tempted to follow his example. The Muslim villagers would strongly disapprove of a liberated young Western woman such as herself travelling in the company of a man who was not her husband. But that wasn't the only reason. Since the events of the night, there was a renewed constraint between herself and Aram and she noticed that he had avoided touching her, or even being close to her if he could put a distance between them. He gave monosyllabic replies to her attempts at conversation, and after a while she gave up trying to be sociable. He looked grim and unshaven, with shadows under his eyes, and the hawk-like face was set in forbidding lines.

There was a simmering sense of unease about him that wasn't a good omen for the rest of the day.

The awkwardness between them lasted for quite a while. Aram drove in silence, his eyes concentrated on the road ahead, but she noticed that this time he kept very much within the speed limit. She didn't know whether it was due to an increase in traffic or her words on the subject the day before, but she didn't care as long as they got to Konya in one piece. From there he intended to take a road that would eventually lead them north to Istanbul. They would have to spend another night somewhere en route, but this time it would be in a hotel. So whatever it was that had put him in such a difficult mood since last night wouldn't have to happen again.

She wondered if it had anything to do with her refusal to let him make love to her. He hadn't seemed particularly upset by it at the time, and she remembered again waking up, tucked close against him with her hand in his. She wondered if he had even been aware of it. Perhaps he had been used to sleeping with a woman...

And that was when a chilling thought struck her. She had been so engrossed by her own determination not to become involved with him that she had never given a passing thought to what his commitments might be. And his quick and open acknowledgement of that attraction between them must also have led her to assume that he was free to pursue her.

He might still regard that pursuit as no more than a game. Just as he made bids for the carpet from time to time, so he made bids for her, and acquiring them both had become a challenge. But with every hour in his company, rows and all, she could feel herself becoming more and more attracted to him, and if he was involved with someone else and still pursuing her, there was a dishonesty about it that turned it from a dangerous little game—dangerous for her, that was—into something quite different.

Impulsively, she turned towards him and it was on the tip of her tongue to ask him if there was a woman in his life. Then she saw that brooding, slightly remote hawk's face, and thought better of it. It would seem such a foolish thing to ask out of the blue like that. Daunted, she looked back to the road, trying to analyse the feelings he evoked in her.

In reality he was only a chance-met stranger who was giving her a lift. They got on quite well when they weren't having a row, and she did find him devastatingly attractive—that aspect seemed to be mutual. But their relationship was developing unevenly. Physically, they were already quite well acquainted, although, if his present reaction meant anything, he might be regretting that. But it didn't alter the fact that she knew very little about him. The eye-patch in the end had turned out to be ridiculously harmless, but what about all that stuff in the back of the car? She still didn't know what he did, where he worked, where he lived, or who he lived with. He might even be married.

Unexpectedly his voice cut across her thoughts. 'What were you going to ask me just now?'

'I—I wasn't going to ask you anything!' she lied. It was just as though he could read her mind.

'Yes you were. What was it?'

She braced herself for the sarcasm she felt sure would follow a question that betrayed so obviously the trend of her thoughts. 'Is there . . . are you—are you married?'

'No.'

'And is there . . . do you have a girlfriend?'

'No. What's prompted this all of a sudden?' He didn't sound surprised, but that was the only thing she could be sure of from that even-toned response.

'I just wondered,' she said awkwardly, and hoped he would leave it at that. He didn't.

'It wouldn't be something to do with last night by any chance, would it?'

She was suddenly afraid he would guess how her nerves were strung as tight as wires. She tried to sound offhand. 'Not really. No.'

But she knew in that instant that something she had just been persuading herself was only a dangerous possibility was already happening. If his answer to either of her questions had been 'yes', then something would have gone out of her life leaving a gap that nothing—and no one—in the future would be able to fill. It was as simple as that.

Despite all her efforts with herself to prevent it, somehow, in only three crazy days, she was falling in love with him.

Whether anything ever came of it or not—and she was almost sure it wouldn't—she would never be again quite the person she was before she met him. She had been right to be cautious: what she could feel for this man, what she felt already, was way beyond anything she might have imagined. She still knew so little about him; he was a man of too few words when it came to his own concerns. But one thing she knew for certain was that no one she'd ever met had had the effect on her that he had, or could do the things to her that he could do. Just when he'd got her absolutely hating him, she found herself seduced into a completely different world by him. One minute she thought him arrogant and dictatorial, and she was squirming under his sarcasm, and the next she was responding to that flashing smile and deep infectious laugh. He had commented on her own straightforwardness, but he could be pretty blunt himself when it suited him—and then withdraw into unexpected silences so that she was afraid she had offended him. She never knew where she was with him.

'You know about my family—what my father used to do, what my brothers do—and you know about my job, the people I work with—even about our business problems,' she added with just a hint of resentment, aware of an unwelcome silence developing between them, and the need to give some neutral explanation for her sudden interest in his personal life. 'That's a lot more than I've discovered about you!' She glanced at him again—and found his eyes already studying her.

If she had hoped that might prompt some instant information from him, she was disappointed. It didn't stop her wondering about him though. Now that she knew there wasn't anybody else in his life, it seemed even more important that she should find out exactly what he did for a living, but as her need to know had increased so had her fear of finding out that some of her earlier speculations about him might prove accurate. She was now afraid to ask. It might be safer for all sorts of reasons not to know—or at least, not to be seen to know... And that gave her food for thought for quite some time.

It was well after midday by the time they reached Konya. They had been held up once by a lorry that had shed its load, and stopped a couple of times for coffee, but before they looked for somewhere to eat Aram was keen to make a phone call.

'It's business,' he said. 'I might have to meet a friend here later if I can contact him to arrange it. Are you coming with me or do you want to wait here? If you go off on your own and get lost, make for Mevlana's mosque, the one with the blue tiles. It's the wrong time of year for dancing Dervishes, but there's lots to look at inside while you're waiting for me to come and find you.'

'Don't worry, I've been here before. But in any case I'll stay in the car.' The last couple of hours' thinking time had given her very good reasons for wanting to be left alone with the car for a while. 'How long will you be?'

'Half an hour?' He raised one dark eyebrow questioningly, as though he wasn't sure she'd agree—it had been a long wait for lunch.

She smiled at him, hoping that on this occasion, at least, he wouldn't be able to read her mind. 'That's fine,' she said. 'Only don't forget about me and go off for lunch on your own—I'm starving.'

His reply left her speechless.

'*Forget about* you, Zelda? When you haven't let me think of anyone—or anything—else for the last forty-eight hours?'

Then he grinned at her, and seconds later was striding off down a side street.

They were parked in a small square that was relatively deserted. There were children playing in one of the alleys that led on to it, and men sitting in a café window that overlooked the square, but no one who would interfere with the plans that had now become obsessional with her. She wished she'd asked Aram exactly where he was going to make his phone call—he seemed to know the town. Maybe some hotel. Half an hour should be long enough . . .

She absolutely *had* to know what was in those boxes. Maybe he'd have told her this time if she'd asked, but if the answer was what she most feared it would be much better to find out for herself and then keep quiet about her knowledge. It was already too late to change her feelings about him, but she could at least prevent any more serious involvement with him by going on to Istanbul alone.

As soon as his tall figure had disappeared from view, she reached into the back of the car. It was impossible to get down to Aram's luggage without unloading her own carpets first. He had left the keys in the ignition, and she hopped out into the square, going round to the hatchback to pull off some of the top layer of rugs.

One of his kitbags was visible underneath, and after hauling out a couple more of her own carpets she managed to pull it up. It was padlocked at the top, and there was no key on the ring that would fit it. She prodded the bag experimentally—it didn't feel as though any metal object were inside...like a gun. But that wasn't much of a consolation. A weapon could be well wrapped up to disguise it. She would have to try something else.

Nervously, aware of the need to get every item she was pulling out neatly back into the car as though it had never been disturbed, she dug deeper and found one of the boxes. It was suspiciously shaped—like a long, flat tea-chest, and the top had been secured all round with small metal tacks. She had seen two other similar boxes when Aram had first loaded the car—this might be her only chance to get a look inside. Unless she splintered the wood while she was trying to prise up a lid, he wouldn't be likely to find out she had opened it once she had secured it again afterwards. It shouldn't take long, and she would only need a few seconds to inspect the contents.

Aware all the time that Aram's half-hour might turn out to be no more than ten minutes, she had a nerve-racking search for a suitable object to use as a lever, until she discovered that part of the wheel-jack in the tool kit had a strong metal edge that was thin enough to slip under the lid. But once she could peer underneath, it was difficult to make out what was inside—some sort of dark covering perhaps... Could there be guns underneath?

In the end she had to prise up the entire box lid. It was going to be a tricky job fitting it back exactly so that the tacks that were still sticking out along the edge could be driven down into the box again, but she would meet that problem when she came to it. She could only pray that Aram's phone call would be a long one. She glanced at her watch—nearly eight minutes had gone by, and the hardest bit—covering up the evidence afterwards—was yet to come.

Once the box lid was up, she reached forward eagerly to touch the greyish canvas that covered whatever it was inside. It was just as well there was no one around. They might suspect she had a body in it... Her heart was suddenly beating so fast it was almost as though she believed her own silly joke. Whatever it was underneath was long and bulky...

She took a deep breath, and quickly twitched the canvas aside. But what was revealed was instantly familiar. The back of a handknotted carpet—quite a large one.

Could it be wrapping something?

She gave a hasty glance around the square, checked her watch—less than half a minute since she last looked, but it had felt like a lifetime!—and began to heave it out. It was very heavy, and bulky. Either it was a very big carpet, or it *was* concealing something. Anyway, it was too late to back out now. She had to find out.

Dumping it down in the road at the back of the car, her own rugs stacked around just as though she'd been setting up some market stall, she gave the mysterious carpet a quick strong flip, unrolling it in front of her.

Then she discovered why it had been so heavy... It was not one carpet but *six!*

They varied in sizes, the smallest being rolled into the middle. And they were all exquisite.

Zelda stared at them as though they had just flown in from Paradise and dropped at her feet of their own accord. Six carpets. Old carpets. Silk carpets... with hundreds of knots to the square inch, and colours so subtle and rich that it was as though the very dyes must be the secret of some long-dead craftsman whose name survived only in legend. Two of them were Turkish, but the others were from Iran. Persian carpets, each one worth a small fortune... The most beautiful carpets she had seen in her life, and Aram had said not one word about them!

There must be more in the car—there were at least two other boxes, and several canvas-wrapped packages. Where had he been—not into Iran, surely? And he had been making determined offers for her paltry little woollen rug which would fetch not one quarter as much as the least valuable of what was now spread out in this Konya backstreet...

'What the *hell* do you think you're doing?'

She spun round, guilt written all over her face, and wished instantly and passionately for an earthquake to open the ground beneath her feet—or preferably those of the tall, strongly built and intimidatingly angry man she had found standing just behind her.

She knew at that moment she had never been quite so nervous of anyone in her life.

She swallowed uncertainly. 'I thought you said half an hour...?' It was the first thing that came into her head.

His eyes had turned that dangerous glass-green that spelt disaster. 'What sort of an explanation is that supposed to be for spreading my carpets across half a dirty square?'

'I...I suppose you're a dealer?' she faltered.

'I am. Come on, Zelda. I'm waiting.'

'I . . . it's . . . well, how was I supposed to know?' she demanded, finally aroused in her own defence. 'Why on earth didn't you *tell* me what you were doing? I thought you were a gun-runner!'

'Bloody hell, Zelda!' He had clearly thought better in that instant of saying something much worse. 'Don't you give that imagination of yours a rest sometimes? Do I look like a gun-runner?'

'As a matter of fact that's just what you do look like!' she countered hotly. 'You look dark and foreign and just like a brigand—and when you had that awful eye-patch I thought you were a terrorist—so there! Normal people don't seem to find it difficult to tell other people what they do for a living, so what was I supposed to think when you wouldn't give me a straight answer?'

'I'm sorry to disappoint you!' There was something threatening just in the way he said that. Zelda gave an involuntary shiver. 'It must be extremely boring after all your colourful ideas to find that I do exactly the same thing as yourself.' The green eyes raked her in a way that made her feel like a twelve-year-old caught going through her father's bank statements. 'Just what did you want precisely—a complete family history—or my unexpurgated autobiography?' She flinched at the sarcasm in his tone. 'I am a carpet dealer, just as my father was, and my grandfather. I've been dealing in carpets since I left school and I spent eight years in Paris working with my uncle—running the business that my grandfather started. Oh, and just in case you wonder what my sister's up to, she doesn't deal in drugs or guns, or anything else your suspicious little mind might think up. She's a perfectly harmless dancer with the Royal Ballet in London. So I'm sorry to have to tell you that we're none of us in the least interested in making any sort of illegal money— all the Kalinskys have quite enough money of their own. Now, what else would you like to know—how many women I've slept with?'

This was excruciating. It was the worst encounter she'd yet had with him and it had to happen in the most public place of all. She could feel her cheeks burning, and couldn't bring herself to meet that angry glare any longer. She was actually afraid of him.

There was a silence. Then he said, 'Now perhaps you'd help me put these back where you found them before we attract a larger audience than the one we've got already.'

Nervously, she glanced away from him to find several little boys watching with eager interest only a few yards away, and the attention of the patrons of the café across the street focused on them.

She bent down to roll the carpets up again. She didn't know quite what she could say. She could sense the anger still pulsing from him.

She took a deep breath, nerving herself for a further outburst. This was so far from his usual laconic style she didn't know what to expect next.

'I'm sorry, Aram, I really am,' she began. 'But you have to admit it was partly your own fault——'

'Just shut up and roll up those carpets. Heaven help you if you've got one drop of oil or tar from the road on them! I'm sorely tempted to leave you here to find your own way to Istanbul.'

He hadn't sounded quite so furious that time, but she didn't dare argue it further. Instead she helped him to lift the heavy roll into its box, and began piling up her own rugs for transfer back into the car. But her feelings of humiliation were beginning to turn into resentment at the injustice of it . . . It *was* his own fault! A carpet dealer, of all things! Why be so mysterious about it? What would have been the harm in admitting to what he did, unless for his own devious reasons he had been trying to get some advantage over her? And the irony of it was now she had established that he was safe to travel with—not being a gun-runner or a terrorist—he was considering leaving her by the roadside!

'Get in,' he ordered curtly, once the entire merchandise had been reloaded.

'But I thought you were going to make a phone call?'

'I couldn't get through.'

'But aren't we going to get anything to eat?'

He gave her that cold look she so disliked. 'With half Konya knowing exactly how valuable the contents of my car are?'

'Turkish people are very honest!' she tried to reason. She was starving, but she wouldn't put it past him now to drive until dark without so much as stopping for coffee.

'Let's not put it to the test just now. Are you coming to Istanbul, or do you want me to dump your stuff back in the road?'

Without another word of protest, she got into the passenger seat, and refrained from slamming the door. It was ironical how last night she had had to fight with herself not to let this man do just what he wanted with her—and now she was wondering how soon she could get out of his company without making her own travel arrangements impossible! How could she have imagined only a few hours ago she was in love with him? She almost hated him!

The more she thought about it, the more angry she got. He had been trying to make a complete fool of her— she remembered now how she had saved up the information about her own dealing in order to get some advantage, and when she had announced it so triumphantly, he had just laughed... No wonder! He was playing exactly the same trick himself. It didn't seem funny to her at all that he had beaten her at her own game.

She stole a glance at him, but the forbidding profile daunted her again.

They left Konya, heading for Afyon, and it was some time before Aram pulled in at a wayside café.

'Still hungry?' He didn't sound as though he'd softened much since the scene in the square, whatever thoughts had occupied his mind for the last forty miles or so.

'Yes,' she said without looking at him.

'We'll stop for half an hour. Repented yet of your evil ways?'

She did look at him then, but with what she hoped was such withering scorn—talk about the pot calling the kettle black!—that she wasn't surprised when the look she received in return was enigmatic.

When they got back into the car after the meal, the atmosphere between them wasn't much better. Zelda found that her spirits had lightened at the prospect of food, but conversation between herself and Aram in the café had been reduced to the minimum, and the only thing she had learned was that he intended to drive as far as possible, so that the last leg of the journey to Istanbul the following day would be relatively short.

She had found herself looking at him once as they munched their way through the pitta envelopes of lemon-sprinkled kebabs and salad, wondering if that grim mouth would show the hint of a smile—the 'daggers drawn' situation was beginning to get her down. Not that she was going to apologise any more than she had already, when she reckoned that he was the one who should now apologise to her for the unreasonable way he had spoken to her, but Aram had caught her staring, and after another of those enigmatic looks had winked at her. She wasn't quite sure how to take that, and no further progress had been made.

She didn't want to risk another row with him if they got back to discussing what had happened in Konya.

CHAPTER SEVEN

'ZELDA, it's nearly eleven o'clock. There's no way I'm driving any further tonight in search of another hotel, which may, or may not have more than one room to rent.' That no-argument tone was unmistakable and she knew at once that it was useless trying to persuade Aram to anything else. 'And I fail to see,' he went on, 'what your objections can be when we shared a room last night.'

The six-room *pansiyon*, in the entrance hall of which they were standing, was the only one they'd passed in miles. She was grateful that the proprietor, a thin elderly Turk sporting a magnificent version of the national moustache, couldn't understand what the heated discussion between his two potential guests was all about.

'That was different!' she protested. 'A freezing cold cave is a long way from being a hotel bedroom with only one bed!' One *double* bed, she added silently.

'Then you can sleep in the car,' he said heartlessly. 'But *I* am definitely going up to the bedroom once you've decided whether or not you're going to play guard-dog to the carpets. If you're not, I'll do something about getting that box you've mangled somewhere safe. Do you want your Turkish rug locked up too?'

Zelda thought fast. A night in the car would be cold and miserable. Since he was the one forcing her into this, he was the one who could sleep on the floor. And she would have her carpet with her—goodness knew what he might have in mind once he got it stored somewhere with his. She hadn't forgotten his promise—or threat— that he would have it in the end. And she hadn't forgotten the other part of that announcement either. He hadn't been so far off winning that part last night.

Briefly, she told him her decision, leaving out the bit about who was to sleep on the floor, and, taking the key to the only room that wasn't already occupied, she headed for the stairs. First she was going to have a shower. Then she'd think about bed.

Aram had been right to call a halt, she had to admit it, and she couldn't accuse him of trying to delay the journey. With one stop on the road for supper, they had driven straight on, until the problem of somewhere to stay had come up. They were too far from any major town to expect a choice of accommodation, and, although he hadn't said anything, she suspected that Aram was every bit as tired as herself—the previous night in the cave hadn't been exactly restful. If there had been two beds in one room, she supposed she mightn't have objected quite so strongly, but with only one...

Diplomatic relations had gradually been restored between them, but not with any marked degree of warmth. There had been no dramatic breakthrough, but rather a gradual thawing process. She had dozed for some of the journey after their break for lunch, which had meant that there was no possibility of conversation, but during supper over a bottle of Turkish wine they had exchanged a few meaningless pleasantries. Aram, however, had made no mention of Konya, and neither had she.

The *pansiyon* turned out to be an old-style private house, with a few new rooms built on to accommodate the guests. Zelda quickly discovered that their much debated 'double' room was in the older part of the building, and, although adequate, was by no means large. A reasonably sized double bed took up most of the floor space; there was a cupboard, an armchair and a table, and an old picture of Kemal Attaturk, founder of modern Turkey, on the wall. The only other feature was the window, constructed in the old-fashioned Turkish style, its wooden grille hung with the dark silhouettes of wisteria leaves. There were going to be problems when it came to who was going to sleep on the only available floor space.

She discovered a shower-room halfway down the passage, and, although the water was only tepid, stood under it revelling in the sensation of being clean at last, until she remembered that Aram too would be waiting to use it. She had brought some fresh clothes with her, and while she put them on—there was no way she was going to undress for bed with Aram around—she thought out her strategy. When he was having a shower, she would get into bed, and possession was nine points of law. Once she had the bed, she wasn't going to share it, but it would hardly come to a physical fight over it. If Aram proved less scrupulous than she had bargained for, then she would just have to get out again.

She refused to let herself dwell on the thought of how, if only she could know he felt as she did, she would like to stay there with him. But she had made up her mind that nothing, absolutely nothing, was going to happen between them.

She should have known that she wouldn't be able to outwit him so easily. She shouldn't have spent so long in the shower—he had found another further along the passage, and as for the nine points of law... She found him in bed when she returned.

Leaning back against the door, she stared at him resentfully. He was lying on one side of the bed, propped on one elbow, his hand behind his head. If he was wearing anything, it wasn't obvious—the sheet was pulled down to his waist. He was looking at her.

'This doesn't say much for your chivalry, does it?' she said accusingly. 'I've told you I'm not getting into bed with you.'

She couldn't read the expression in his eyes. 'In any other circumstances, I might be tempted to be chivalrous, but not now. Not with you.'

'Why not?' she demanded, secretly rather hurt as well as annoyed. What was so different about her that she failed to inspire his chivalry, only his more selfish instincts? Despite all her resolutions, even in the unromantic light of the single bulb in the middle of the ceiling, she couldn't help being acutely aware of the sculptured lines of that muscular body, and the dusting of dark hair across his chest, that tapered down below his waist...

Embarrassed by the trend of her thoughts, she looked away quickly, conscious that he was still studying her, those strange light eyes suddenly speaking a very direct message.

'Because we've been playing games one way or another since the first moment we met, and I've decided it's time to stop. Last night I discovered that you want me just as much as I want you, only for some reason you won't admit it. Why won't you be honest? I want you very much, Zelda.'

'*You've* decided...!' She was completely taken aback by the directness of the attack, and also by his assumption that she would automatically see things his way. This wasn't what she'd been expecting at all—and to think that it had even crossed her mind to offer another apology for what had happened in Konya, in the hope that it would improve relations between them the following morning! But she'd been imagining herself making her magnanimous offer from a position of strength—secure possession of the bed... 'I don't see why that should stop you offering to sleep on the floor!' she argued illogically, trying to gather her wits. It was fine being honest about sexual attraction if that was all it amounted to, but in her case things were far more complicated. Yes, he wanted her, but where did her own confused feelings fit in? 'I'd have thought it would be very good for your...lust...or whatever it is,' she finished lamely.

'Why retire defeated when I could have it all—the bed and you?'

So now finally she'd come up against that unscrupulous streak she'd always suspected was in him, but it didn't change the way she felt about him. 'Are you serious about this, Aram?' she asked quietly.

'I'm serious about wanting you—and about not sleeping on the floor.' He sounded unnervingly dispassionate about it. 'You're free to decide what to do about it. You can come to bed with me and I won't even touch you, if that's what you'd really prefer—or *you* can sleep on the floor with your beloved rug.'

'You were talking about playing games just now,' she said bitterly. 'Why do you keep making bids for that rug? You're a dealer—you know it's not worth as much as all that, not in comparison with the sort of thing you've bought.'

There was a moment's hesitation before he spoke. 'Because it's a game.'

'And I suppose that's why you want me?' she pursued, not bothering to disguise the hurt in her voice.

'No,' he said quietly. 'I've never been the sort of man who takes a woman just because she's a challenge.'

'Why do you want me, then?'

He met her eyes steadily. 'I've told you—there's been something between us since the first moment we met. You fascinate me. I can't stop thinking about you. You're different from any girl I've ever met.'

'And I suppose you've met hundreds.' The sarcasm was very pointed.

'Met, yes, probably. I travel a lot. But what you mean is lovers, isn't it?' He didn't wait for her reply, but there was a quirk of humour in the corner of his mouth. 'My autobiography again? I assure you Zelda, there have been very few. After the last one, I didn't think ... I wasn't going to ...' For the first time since she had met him, he sounded hesitant.

'What?' she asked quickly. Here was something, at last, that might give her a new glimpse of the man behind all the images she had constructed round him—images that had so far proved misleading.

'Get involved with anyone else.'

'Why? What went wrong?'

There was a self-deprecating twist to his mouth now when he spoke. 'The old story. She decided she liked someone else better than me.'

He didn't add any more, and there was silence while they weighed each other up, the distance of the room between them.

'Tell me,' she said at last. If it wasn't a game, then it was time he proved it.

He gave an impatient sigh. 'There's not very much that's relevant . . . except that I fell in love with her when we first met. The attraction seemed to be mutual and we were together for about six months—until she decided she liked my best friend better than me. I'd wanted to marry her, but she'd seemed determined to keep her independence, and then she married him within weeks. There was a lot of deception and self-deception going on all round. It ended up unhappily for everyone. She and my friend split up in less than a year.'

Her next question was tentative; if she pushed too hard, he might clam up altogether. 'Were you very much in love with her?'

'Yes.'

In some ways, the story was familiar. Parts of it could be her story too. Reading between the lines, she guessed that his determination not to get involved with anyone else showed he must have been badly hurt by the woman, whoever she was.

'How long ago was that?'

'Three years. Don't waste your sympathy. I got over it.'

It didn't sound as though he had, if after all that time he was still resisting involvement with anyone else. Or perhaps it had just made him extra wary, as her own experience should have made her. That reflection should have strengthened what was left of her weakening resolution—it would be too easy to give in because she imagined they shared the trauma of a painful love-affair.

He wasn't an easy man to get to know, but, despite his last words, her ready sympathy reached out to him.

'How old are you, Aram?'

'Thirty. Why?' He sounded surprised.

'It's not important.' But it was important, to her. The continuing determination of an experienced man of thirty not to involve himself in further love-affairs, was a very different thing from an impulsive and emotional re-action to the same kind of disappointment had he been a twenty-year-old.

'You must have cared about her very much if you weren't willing to get involved with anyone else,' she commented.

He shrugged. It was impossible to tell whether the offhand gesture showed a genuine lack of feeling, or not. 'I fell for Gina very fast—I didn't want the same sort of thing to happen again. I don't want it to happen to us.'

A warning—or a rejection? 'Am I like her?'

He gave a sideways smile. 'I don't think there's much similarity between you and a five-foot-ten redhead.'

'There might be in other ways...'

'Like a bad temper?' he suggested.

'Speak for yourself!' she countered instantly, but there was no real humour in the exchange. She needed time to think about what he'd told her, and what it might say about his feelings for her.

'Well, have you decided?' he asked, after a silence. She knew what he was referring to, and hardened her resolution. 'You actually seem to believe that I'm going to find the prospect of cold-blooded sex an attractive one!' Determinedly, she crossed to get her rug from beside the wardrobe, where he had propped it. He watched her spread it on the floor, and then shake out a spare blanket.

'What happened in the cave didn't seem very cold-blooded to me—and I can't see you spending the whole night on a draughty floor with spiders, just to prove a point.'

She didn't like the mention of spiders—nor did she like the way he had remembered her weaknesses. How typical of him to make such unscrupulous use of the knowledge! Deliberately she fuelled her sense of grievance. While she was angry with him, there was no danger of finding herself in his bed.

She took off her jeans, but kept on her underwear and T-shirt, and a pair of long socks.

Aram was lying back now, propped up on the pillows, his hands behind his head. 'Aren't you going to get undressed?' She thought he sounded lazy and comfortable, and she could have hit him.

'I am undressed,' she said shortly, aware of his eyes following her as she crossed to the door to switch out the overhead light. Then she made her way back to crawl into the blanket.

October could be chilly at night, and he had been right about the draughts. Her feet began to get very cold.

It was easy enough to keep up the strength of her convictions while she could persuade herself she was angry with him, but what seemed like hours later she was still awake in the half-dark. It was too like a repetition of the night before, but this time she wouldn't give in—she *wouldn't*!

Her legs were cold, her feet felt like blocks of ice, she kept wondering about spiders, and not for one minute— despite everything—would her body let her forget that Aram was only a few feet away, and that he wanted her every bit as much as she wanted him.

She began to think about his past involvement with a woman who had left him. She knew all about the feelings of betrayal and hurt pride that that could involve. She remembered how desolate she had felt when Dan left her, and how empty life had seemed once she had come to terms with the fact. Her new interest in the Magic Carpets Company at that time had played a vital part not only in filling that dreadful gap in her existence, but in building back her confidence again. She wondered how many of her past feelings Aram might share—clearly he wasn't going to tell her even if she asked.

He had told her that she filled his thoughts, that she fascinated him, that he wanted to know her better, and had admitted that he had been wary of any further involvement. If he wanted her so much now, surely it couldn't be only the lust she had half accused him of— simple lust didn't lead to involvement. It was love, even unrecognised love, that did. If he was afraid of involvement with her, then he was afraid of loving her. And if he was afraid of loving her then it was because he was afraid of betrayal. But she felt as though she was already committed to him, a commitment that had begun literally within hours of their first meeting, with that disturbing kiss out in the wilds of the Syrian desert.

If she was going to make a mistake, then it was the worst mistake she had ever made. But she was sure now she loved him—each discovery she made about him only increased that sureness...

She got up off the floor, still wrapped in her blanket, and stood, hesitating, beside the bed—now that the moment had come it was the old battle between head and heart, and she knew she was letting her emotions get the better of her.

'What's the matter?' His voice was very low and quiet, but so unexpected it almost made her jump. She saw his eyes glitter in the dark as he turned towards her.

So he hadn't been asleep either, despite the bed! 'Nothing.' Then, 'My feet are cold.'

'Come here and I'll warm them up for you.'

She wondered if he understood what she hadn't found the courage to say, and sat down gingerly on the edge of the mattress. It tilted a little under her, as he shifted his weight.

'Put your feet up here. That's better.'

She felt a touch on her knee, and then he was stripping off her socks, and taking one foot in his hands. His fingers were enticingly warm.

'Cold as virtue,' he commented drily. 'Had enough of the floor?'

'Aram—don't!' She couldn't bear one of his sarcastic moods now. She didn't want this to be the outcome of one of those games between them—then she would despise herself afterwards for being so easily won.

Her feet were coming back to tingling life, and when she felt his hand slide round her ankle and up the side of her leg in a gentle caress she moved so that she could look down at him. He was half lying beside her, propped on one elbow, and he reached out to touch her cheek, and then run his fingers back through her hair, pushing the silky strands back from her face.

'I just wish you'd tell me why you think it's such a bad idea to let me make love to you,' he said softly. 'Don't you like sex?'

'It's not that,' she whispered. She could only be honest with him now that they had got this far. Perhaps it would be the one sure way of turning him off and that would take all need for a decision from her. 'It's just ... well, to me it's love, and I can't—I don't want to—separate the two. I always get too emotionally involved too quickly, and then it's a disaster.'

'Which—the sex or the relationship?'

'The relationship,' she admitted reluctantly. She was shivering, but it was no longer because of her exile on the floor. He wasn't touching her now, and she wondered if what she had just said had changed his mind.

'Which particular relationship were you thinking of?' he asked gently.

She took a while to answer. 'Like you, there was somebody I ... cared about very much. I'd never slept with anyone before Dan, and it meant such a lot. Then he went back to his girlfriend—he'd been seeing her all along, but I didn't know. It hurt so much I didn't want that sort of involvement again.' It wasn't talking about Daniel she found so difficult—it was wondering all the while if he understood what she was telling him about her own feelings for him. 'Making love is...is a language,' she faltered. 'It's no good if you haven't got anything to say...'

'And do you think we've got anything to say to each other?' he asked slowly.

'I don't know.' This was agony. With her body screaming awareness of him, all she wanted was for him to take her in his arms and show her whatever it was he wouldn't put into words.

'Then maybe it's time to find out?'

But he didn't move. He seemed almost detached about it, as though it were some sort of experiment.

'Take your clothes off,' he said quietly. 'I have to be sure you really want this.'

She knelt up on the bed awkwardly, pulling off her shirt, and then unfastened the catch of her bra. She had thought he would do it, stripping her clothes off her in the sort of passion that would take all decision from her. This was almost too cold-blooded.

When she was naked she lay back on the bed beside him, waiting for him to make a move. There was an eternity while he looked down at her, and she wondered if he had changed his mind. Had he really understood what she had just told him? Doubts crept in... Her 'I don't know' could have meant she was unsure of her own feelings, just as much as of the nature of the relationship itself. As far as she was concerned, he was the unknown quantity, not she. Perhaps he was doing this just to humiliate her after she had fought him off so determinedly. She had done as he asked, and she couldn't have shown him more clearly that she had made up her mind. She was shivering violently now. 'Aram, please. Hold me,' she begged. 'I can't bear this.'

At last he touched her, tracing the line of her cheek with one finger, and then the fullness of her underlip.

She smiled with sheer relief, and bit him, and then
quickly turned her lips into the palm of his hand, longing
for him to take her in his arms.

She heard him laugh, a low, warm laugh that somehow
reassured her, and his voice when he spoke had that
familiar deep edgy note. 'If making love is a language,
my little carpet dealer, then I've got plenty to say to you.
It could take all night...'

Then there was nothing relaxed, or experimental,
about the feel of him when without warning he moved.
His muscles were as tense as hers, and he was already
fully aroused as he pulled her against him, pressing the
length of his thighs against hers, his arms tight round
her waist and back so that her breasts ached against the
wall of his chest. The sensation of his hair-roughened
limbs against her own smooth skin was infinitely erotic,
and as his mouth claimed hers with an impatience that
literally took her breath away her body took fire.

She felt as though she were melting, turning to liquid
in the heat that swept through her, and clung to him as
her only solid anchor in that intense and dizzying world.
She dug her nails into his shoulders, her response to his
plundering mouth betraying a passion she had never experienced before. But, although caught up in an all-
engulfing tide, she seemed still aware of every separate
inch of him, and as his hand travelled quickly down her
side, feverishly caressing first her breast and then her
thigh and sparking a thousand individual responses from
every nerve-end, she moved wantonly against him, desperate for the moment of his possession.

He broke the contact of their mouths, breathing rag-
gedly. 'Zelda—darling—slow down...' His half-whisper
was hoarse and unsteady, as though he was already on
the verge of losing the control he was trying to exercise
over her. 'We've got all the rest of the night.'

Despite the unexpected endearment, a flood of shame
washed through her—what on earth must he think of
her? She'd told him that she got involved too quickly,

but this hadn't been what she had meant at all. It had never, ever happened to her like this before. She gave a little moan, and tried to turn her head away, too embarrassed to look at him, even in the near darkness. 'I'm sorry—I—I didn't mean...'

'Ssh, it's all right,' he reassured her, his voice more like the familiar low growl now. 'You do the same to me.'

Strong fingers under her chin forced her to turn towards him again, and she saw the glitter of his eyes, before his lips touched hers with a new gentleness.

She was aware that they were in a small hotel room, and that the sounds they made could probably be heard through the walls if there was anyone still awake in the early hours of the morning. But it wasn't long before they were caught up again in the same maelstrom, mutual need this time sweeping all control away. They came together quickly and violently, Zelda tasting her own blood as she bit her lips to stop herself crying out as he took her. The climax was almost instantaneous, and as she felt him gasp and stiffen above her, she seemed to fall from a great height deep into widening rings of an endless pleasure that was herself and Aram together, somewhere beyond time.

How long they lay like that, she didn't know. But, as she slowly swam back up to consciousness, she knew that something new had happened to her. If making love was a language, as she had told Aram, then it seemed to her that what they had had to say to each other had been something momentous. There had never been a time to pretend that her emotions weren't involved—what had just taken place had been inevitable from the moment they had met.

Aram had been a challenge to her from the beginning—fascinating her, scaring her a little, and always one jump ahead. As an individual, he was the most magnetic person she had ever encountered, with that aura of power and hint of danger that hovered round him, even when he was at his most sociable; as a friend—well, she had yet to test that.

She still found it difficult to read him; most of the time he revealed just so much of himself as he chose. She wondered now if the sarcasm that had been a little hard to take wasn't purely defensive. His admission earlier about his unsuccessful relationship had surprised her. He could be a great deal more vulnerable than she had imagined. And in his dealings with her she couldn't really find much to complain of: he'd been helpful, kind when it mattered, and, apart from the uneasiness between them that had arisen for quite other reasons, good to get along with.

And as for that uneasiness...everything would be well now they had given in to the mutual attraction that had been between them from the very first, an attraction which had turned out to be so much more powerful than she had ever imagined at the beginning. Surely it wasn't unreasonable to hope that he might have made the same discovery?

She could feel his breath on her neck, quiet and even now that the violent pulse in them both had been stilled. She could feel too the moth-wing brushing of his lashes against her cheek so that she knew his eyes were open and he was awake.

Finally he stirred, moving a little apart, and, slipping an arm under her, drew her against him, her head on his shoulder.

'You're wonderful, Zelda,' he whispered. 'Did you know that?' Again she felt his breath stir her hair, and then his lips touched her forehead.

She should have been satisfied with the compliment—no one had ever called her that before. But she couldn't help the pang of disappointment because he had said nothing about his feelings for her, and whether what they had just shared had changed them in any way. Why couldn't he have told her what she had tried to tell him—that what they felt for each other was love?

She ran her hand lightly down his arm, and when she touched his fingers, linked her own through his. He squeezed them, pulling her a little closer, and then relaxed, on the very edge of sleep.

She lay awake a while longer, her body at peace but her mind still restless. Why did it always have to happen like this? Some women might be capable of giving just their bodies—which was all, it seemed, that most men wanted—but stupid Zelda Denton, who never learned, always had to give her heart...

They made love again in the early morning, to the twittering of sparrows outside in the old wooden grilles that screened their window. She had been awakened by Aram, slowly surfacing from a deep sleep to the seductive claims her body was already making on her, and turning willingly towards him. There was less desperate urgency this time, but the end when it came seemed just as uncontrollable and overwhelming, and they fell easily into sleep once more still in each other's arms.

The drive to Istanbul the following morning was in marked contrast to the day before. There was none of that strained atmosphere between them that had stemmed from her mistrust of him, and led to the incident in Konya that had blighted much of the subsequent journey.

If there was anything about the relationship now that Zelda was unhappy with, it concerned a disappointment she couldn't reason away, that, despite a night which for her had been a revelation of some of her deepest feelings, Aram hadn't said anything about his own. Sex, however perfect, had its drawbacks as a language, she told herself wryly—it only worked effectively when you had in advance one or two vital clues as to what exactly you were being told. It was true that their 'conversation' had taken up much of the night, but the one thing she had wanted so desperately to know it hadn't told her.

Most of the journey passed in a sort of glorious haze. They didn't talk much, but Aram once stopped the car by a deserted stretch of road only to take her in his arms and kiss her with a leisurely thoroughness that made her wish they were back in that long-argued-over bed, with all the early hours of the morning left to them.

'How long have you got in Istanbul before your flight?' he asked at last, brushing a strand of hair behind her ear. 'Or do I have to take you straight to the airport?'

'Two days,' she admitted somewhat shamefacedly, and waited for the reaction.

There was a stunned silence. 'You mean I've been going like a bat out of hell because you told me you only had about three days, and you've had longer all the time?'

'N-no. Not exactly.' She felt rather ashamed that her earlier 'insurance' strategy had to be revealed after what had so recently happened between them.

'Then *what* exactly?' It was obvious he saw through her.

She gave him that well-practised look out of wide grey eyes. This was one man she had yet to find out if it would work on. She couldn't be sure of his expression for a moment, and then to her relief he began to laugh.

'You really are incredible! Just when I think I've got you worked out, there's another trick up your sleeve. You're even more wily than I gave you credit for.' But it didn't sound as though he disapproved.

'You're not mad at me?'

He began to trace the line of her cheek with one finger. 'Why should I be mad at you for being a particularly clever little carpet dealer? I admire you very much—or didn't I make that sufficiently clear last night?'

She smiled but refused to meet his eyes. 'I didn't think *admiration* had that much to do with it! But I didn't mean to lie about my flight, honestly. It was just that I didn't trust you at first, and afterwards it slipped my mind.'

'Yes. I was a gun-runner. What other possibilities went through that wild little mind of yours?'

'Dope smuggler...terrorist?' she offered.

'And do you trust me now?' His thumb under her chin, he tilted her face, forcing her to look at him.

She wanted to say I would if I knew you loved me, but they'd had that discussion last night, and what was there to add to it this morning?

'I'm thinking about it!' Her teasing tone made light of the truth behind that statement.

She hadn't given much thought to what was going to happen when they reached Istanbul. She knew the city quite well, and was used to staying in a small hotel not far from the main tourist sights of the old town. It was cheap and convenient, and had proved helpful in the past over difficulties with her carpets. There was still the problem of transporting so many, but if the worst came to the worst she might be able to arrange to leave them at the hotel to be picked up by one of Mehmet's contacts.

She wasn't used to having to go along with someone else's decision, but this time she was happy to let Aram solve all the problems—particularly when his plans involved two nights at the Hilton.

'But I can't afford to stay here!' she protested at his first suggestion. 'I thought you said we were only coming in here for a drink—I'm supposed to be making money for Magic Carpets, not spending it!'

'You're not going to be spending it. You're staying here with me. Or are you tired of me already?'

She looked across at him where he was sitting in one of the wide, comfortable armchairs in the smart international bar in which they were having a drink. There seemed nothing predatory now about that familiar hawk face, and she had to quell an impulse to cross to him and sit in his lap and run her fingers through that crisp blue-black hair. Instead, she smiled into his eyes.

'You know I'm not,' she said quietly.

They had dinner at the hotel. If their surroundings lacked the authentic excitement of some of the city restaurants, they made up for it in luxury, and when finally they went up to their room that night, there was no argument this time over who was to sleep in the vast double bed.

'I've been waiting to be alone with you like this ever since we got up this morning,' Aram said, as she went willingly into his arms.

Perhaps, in the two days he had to spend with her, he would become more certain about his feelings for her. But two days wasn't very long...

They spent the next day exploring the bazaar, and revisiting their favourite mosques. In the early evening, Aram took her to some gardens high above the city where they drank tea in the little marble kiosks that were set among the lawns and trees. Below them, Istanbul spread out like a jewel casket, its lights glittering in the dusk.

'I've been to this city lots of times, but I've never seen it quite this way before,' Zelda said at last. It was almost as though breaking the silence between them would cause all the mysterious beauty to vanish.

'That's because you've never been here with me,' he said, and kissed her.

Her response was without thought. 'It's because I've never been here before with the man I love!'

Suddenly, there was a different kind of silence, and she knew somehow she shouldn't have said it. But it was too late, and she had to go on. 'Aram, you know how I feel about you—why can't you tell me what you feel for me?'

He didn't answer immediately, but put his arms round her, pulling her close so that her face was against his shirt.

She waited. 'Aram...?'

When he spoke, his voice sounded rough and uneven, but in a way she hadn't heard before. 'Zelda, I know what you want to hear, but I can't say it—not yet. It's too soon to know for certain what we feel for each other.'

He was holding her so tightly she could hardly breathe. She wished she could see his face.

'Is this—is this something to do with that woman you told me about?'

'Gina? I don't know. Perhaps.'

She felt his fingers sliding up into her hair, and he pulled her head back gently so that she was looking up at him. His eyes, very green, fringed by thick dark lashes, searched hers.

'You're not an easy person to get to know, are you?' she said carefully, after a pause. And then tried to ease some of the tension between them. 'You wouldn't even tell me what you did for a living...!'

To her surprise there was an awkward silence, and the dark brows were suddenly drawn together in a quick frown. When he spoke she had the weirdest feeling that it wasn't what he had been going to say. 'So what do you think now I've been revealed as a rival carpet dealer?'

'I don't see us as rivals,' she said, slowly. 'Not any more, anyway. Are you a very successful carpet dealer?'

Somehow, they were never far from the subject of carpets, and for her there was still the problem of how to get her own purchases back to England. That was one difficulty that wasn't going to go away just because she was ignoring it for a while.

'Yes. Very!' The new teasing note in his voice was somehow unconvincing. There was something almost careful now about the way he was choosing his words. 'Not so long ago we—that is, Kalinsky's—took over another similar dealer's in London. Ever heard of anyone called Marten and Palmer?'

She thought about it. They were one of the oldest established dealer's in England—small, but well respected.

'That sounds extremely ambitious!' she commented, cautiously. What exactly was he telling her—or maybe *not* telling her? Kalinsky's of Paris must be a bigger concern than she'd been prepared to believe.

He smiled fleetingly, his thumb idly caressing the line of her jaw. 'And you're not ambitious, with your three-person company and phenomenal turnover?' But before she could reply, he went on, 'How would you feel if Magic Carpets became part of some bigger concern? Suppose you could still go on doing your job, but somebody else took over the management of the company?'

'I guess I'd hate it,' she admitted. 'I've already told you it's important to me—to all three of us—that Magic Carpets makes it on its own. But I couldn't bear being dictated to by some know-all businessman behind an office desk, who knew nothing about what he was selling but the numbers on the price tags. Admittedly, Melanie and Rick don't know all that much either, but at least they don't tell me what to do. It's the freedom I need— and that's one of the vital ingredients of that "romance" we talked about. I love what I do—I don't want it to change!'

Somehow, in the middle of all that, she had grown quite impassioned, and her little speech was greeted by an unnerving silence. She was no longer sure now what they were talking about.

'I thought you understood,' she said a little sadly.

'I do, Zelda. We're two of a kind.'

'Then why can't you——?'

He seemed to know she was going to ask him again for the commitment it was so difficult for him to put into words, and he interrupted her. 'Listen, Zelda,' he said quietly, 'I don't find it easy to analyse my feelings, or to talk about them. I never have. And at this moment I don't really know what I feel...except that you're very important to me. I want you with me—I don't want you to go back to London. I want you to talk to—to make love to——'

'That's just sex.' She couldn't keep the note of bitterness out of her voice; just when she was hoping that he might be ready to acknowledge what he felt, it seemed they had never moved off square one.

'No, it isn't, and I think you know it perfectly well. But I don't want to talk about this now. Don't let's spoil the time that's left—don't let's create a problem in the one thing that could be straightforward between us.'

But it isn't straightforward! she wanted to protest. It isn't straightforward at all! But she didn't really understand what he was trying to tell her.

She reached up to pull his head down to her so that she could kiss him. His mouth on hers was very gentle, and she realised, even as she responded to him, that although in the past it was something he had done with passion, he had never before kissed her with such tenderness. It was almost as though he was trying to comfort her for something he couldn't give her.

They walked for a while among the dark trees, both preoccupied, Zelda with thoughts of Aram she couldn't now put into words. Later they went back down into the city, and had dinner in one of the backstreets—almost the whole alleyway had been turned into a vast restaurant. There were gypsy musicians wandering between the closely packed tables, and afterwards Aram stole the rose off the table they had been sitting at and gave it to her. The gesture was probably no more than a joke, but she wondered if he'd guess that she'd keep it.

Her last day in Istanbul was just as dreamlike. This time they walked in the gardens of the fabled Topkapi palace, and sat in the sun looking over the Bosphorus—the stretch of sea beyond the Sultan's palace that divided the Western world from the mysterious East. Later they made their way through the streets again, past the shoe-shine boys on every corner, dodging the pedlars and money changers. In one narrow alley, not far from the palace, they met a man with a bear.

Despite that intense, rather puzzling conversation she had had with him in the gardens, Zelda began to feel that on some deep, mysterious level they were in tune with each other, anticipating each other's thoughts, and sharing the same humour. Perhaps this was what he had meant when he had talked of what was straightforward between them.

It was something she remembered long afterwards—like a dream.

It wasn't until the last morning that the question of carpets came up once more, but in a way that threatened to destroy the idyll that she and Aram had created, reminding her of her insecurity and the need that had now become almost desperate with her, for some sort of commitment from him.

The carpets, brought up from the hotel safe, were heaped all round them in the bedroom, and she had been wondering if she should try to sort them. He had suggested that he should take all her rugs back to England with him in the car. It had seemed at first an ideal way out of her difficulty.

'If I could I'd keep you here with me,' he'd said persuasively, 'then we could both travel back together overland—are you sure you can't stay?'

They'd already discussed that possibility and dismissed it. It might add as much as two weeks on to her travel time, and she was working to a tight schedule. She'd promised Melanie she'd be back on the date she'd given her, and it was vital that at least some of the carpets reached the warehouse as soon as possible.

She shook her head, concentrating on the mess on the floor, and then he said, 'So I'll take the rugs back for you.' And then added a comment that was clearly meant as a joke, but, ironically, sowed seeds of real doubt. 'That is if you're sure that you can trust me!'

It was at that moment that she realised the decision was not wholly hers to take—the carpets belonged to Melanie and Rick as much as to her. She had a right to do what she wished with her own possessions, but not with theirs. But it seemed such an insult after what had happened between herself and Aram, she couldn't look at him as she suggested a compromise that would halve the risk—if there was one. 'I have to take some of them,'

she said evasively. 'We've got to have something worthwhile to sell, and quickly—like *now*! We can't afford to
wait for you to bring it all home.'

He didn't comment immediately, watching her as she
squatted down to begin sorting the rugs. Perhaps he
guessed from her manner more than her words what was
going on in her mind. And the sorting process wasn't
lost on him either—she was making a little collection of
what was most valuable.

There was a heavy silence, and then he said quietly,
'You really don't trust me, do you?'

'It's not my risk!' she protested without looking up,
glad that her hair had swung forward to hide her face.
Foolishly, she didn't choose her words. 'These carpets
are Melanie's and Rick's—I've got no right to entrust
them to a complete stranger——'

'I'd hardly say we're strangers after last night—or the
night before—or the night before that, would you?' That
cutting edge of sarcasm was back in his voice, and she
winced.

'You know what I mean.'

He looked down at her steadily, until she was forced
to meet his gaze. His eyes were hard.

'Yes,' he said. 'I think I do.'

'Aram——' If it had been anyone less self-contained,
less sure of himself than this man, she would have said
she had just hurt him, very much.

'Are you sure you can trust me with the rubbish?' he
demanded harshly. 'That's what you've got in mind, isn't
it?'

'You know it's not like that!'

Then the green ice seemed to thaw a couple of de-
grees, and without warning he reached down, catching
her by the arms to pull her up against him. Her face was
buried in the front of his shirt, and he rested his chin
on her hair. His voice was ragged. 'Zelda, I'm crazy
about you—I've been crazy about you since the first
moment I saw you.'

She stood perfectly still. She felt suddenly stabbed with guilt. She had told him she loved him, and now he was asking her to trust him she wasn't going to—which was as good as saying she didn't really love him at all. She was astonished to discover just how much she could hurt him. Earlier in their relationship her remarks might have sparked a full-scale row, unless she had decided to endure his sarcasm, but this admission from him was perhaps the nearest she was going to get to what she had been wanting to hear.

'Crazy' about her. Yes, but that didn't mean he loved her. It was a treacherous phrase, even if he didn't mean it as such: if he'd been crazy about her from the moment he saw her, then it was before he could have known the first thing about her. She could have been anything—an absolute bitch, for all he knew... Perhaps that was what he was afraid of. He had been hurt before, and he was afraid she might not turn out to be everything he had thought.

He was aware of her long indecision, reading it accurately. But his next words were completely unexpected. 'You're right,' he said with an unmistakable bitterness. 'We are still strangers. We know each other's bodies, but not each other's minds. It's hard to realise we've only been together for a few days. We've quarrelled a lot, but we haven't really talked enough. I haven't found it easy to——' He broke off. 'There are still some gaps in this relationship we're going to have to bridge if we're getting anywhere at all. Are you going to trust me with *anything*?'

She lifted her head from his chest to look up at him. The ice had completely melted now, but what she saw in his eyes this time she wasn't sure she could interpret.

She reached up, putting her arms round his neck, and on impulse said, 'You can take my Turkish carpet...' She could hardly have offered more convincing proof of trust in any circumstances.

He smiled down into her eyes, but, as his mouth closed over hers and she gave herself up to the long kiss, she couldn't help wondering about the wisdom of what she had done...

CHAPTER EIGHT

ASKED to guess at what might have happened at home in her absence, Zelda would never, she told herself on Monday morning, never in a million years have hit on the right answer. Her euphoria, about Aram, Istanbul—everything!—had lasted just as long as it had taken her to fly home on Sunday afternoon, and get herself and her carpets to the warehouse first thing the following day.

'The warehouse', impressive-sounding though it was, comprised a building about the size of a double garage, which they had been lucky enough to acquire leasehold from a friend of Melanie's. It cost them a lot of money, but it was conveniently situated and it was there that they stacked and packed the carpets after the washing process that was carried out at Melanie's house. It was from the warehouse that they made their sales, and there they had installed all the trappings of a mini-office, including a phone.

An attempt to call Melanie at home the night before had proved unsuccessful. But now she discovered that far from being out enjoying herself, as she had expected, her partner had spent dismal hours at the local police station.

She should have guessed from her first sight of Rick that something was wrong. The warehouse doors were wide open, and he had been half slouched against the doorframe, arms crossed, staring dolefully at the scuffed toes of his trainers—he'd got his carpet-shifting gear on, but there was not a glimmer of his usual lively enthusiasm. Melanie, sitting on a pile of rugs inside, a pen and paper in her hands, looked a picture of unrelieved gloom.

The thing that did strike her as odd immediately was the fact that the pile of rugs Melanie had chosen to sit on was the only pile of rugs in the entire warehouse.

They both looked up as she appeared, lugging a couple of carpets. She'd been forced to park her battered Renault a street away.

'Hey—you two! What's happened to our stock? Had a phenomenal selling binge—or has someone pinched it?' It was easy to be flippant about such things when you'd just come back from two days' romantic dream in Istanbul, and the only thing you thought there was in the world to worry you was that the man you were so desperate about didn't love you the way you loved him... And then something about the looks that came over both faces got through to her.

'I... I've just brought you some wonderful bargains...' she went on feebly. 'Isn't anybody interested?'

Melanie had stared at her as though she was the last person on earth she expected to see. Had she actually *forgotten* about her? Zelda couldn't help wishing now she'd taken a chance and stayed behind with Aram—so much for a sense of responsibility to your friends!

Melanie was a couple of years older than Zelda, and, despite her untidy and rather downbeat appearance, had a good head for business, and if there could be said to be a 'boss' in the company, then she was it. Both Rick and Zelda respected her judgement, although Zelda could have wished she'd be just a little more adventurous at times.

Like Zelda she had dark hair, but, whereas Zelda's page-boy cut never looked anything but neat, Melanie's long straggling locks were usually gathered into a haphazard pony-tail that had a suggestion of punk about it—she had once dyed the ends the sort of red that bordered on a dull vermilion. She could have been very striking, with her height and her pale skin and eyes, but in Zelda's opinion she never made anything of her looks. She tended to dress in leather jackets and jeans that lacked the charm and style they took on when Zelda wore them.

Then Melanie's expression changed, and Zelda didn't need her confirmation of it to guess that something in what she'd just said hadn't been too wide of the mark.

'Is that all you've brought back after two months?' she said dismally. 'Because unless they're going to fetch five figures, we'll be out of work before the end of the week.'

Zelda looked from one to the other of her partners. 'Isn't somebody going to tell me what's happened?'

'I'd have thought it was self-evident,' Rick said shortly. He looked thoroughly depressed. 'Ever known us to sell *every single carpet* in two months?'

'It's possible,' she said non-committally.

'We've had a burglary.' It was Melanie this time. 'The whole lot just vanished overnight.'

Zelda knew now, very suddenly, what the phrase about having the stuffing knocked out of you meant. She let her armful of carpets sag to the ground.

'What about the rugs you're sitting on?' she said weakly.

'These are what I had at home—some of them were being washed and we hadn't got round to delivering the rest back here.' They'd always known they should have the locks renewed, and that the few extra padlocks they'd put on the warehouse doors as a concession to the insurance company wouldn't deter a professional thief. Someone must have known what was inside.

Rick pulled a face, running a hand through sandy-coloured hair. 'We think it must have happened some time during the early hours of Sunday morning. I came in yesterday by chance, and found the place a mess—stuff from the desk spread all over the floor—someone must have up-ended the drawers—and the telephone ripped out.'

Zelda seemed to have left her wits somewhere back in Istanbul. It was difficult to adjust. 'We are fully insured?' She hardly dared listen for the answer.

'As long as they don't make any difficulties about that "new locks" clause in the agreement. But we need cash *now*—not next month, or next year.'

'Melanie's going through a list of the stock for the police and the insurance but it took all yesterday to get the papers back into any sort of order.'

How *could* it have happened? Just when it had looked as though everything was getting better for them! Of course, they had had a few money problems, but the company had really looked as though it might be getting somewhere at last. And now this!

Grimly, they discussed the details of the stolen stock, and speculated on the burglary until Rick suddenly said, in an effort to be cheerful, 'So what have you brought us from Turkey that's going to reverse our fortunes? Let's have a look at all the goodies—are they in the car?'

'Some of them,' she said a little cautiously. She knew her partners might not regard her arrangement with Aram as a particularly bright idea, even if she had extracted the more valuable purchases first. And although she had spent most of the flight in a state of euphoria over the tall dark-haired man she had said such a passionate goodbye to at the airport, and wondering how she was going to get through one day without him—let alone two weeks—she had given some thought to the problem of her explanation, and how she was going to make what she had done sound her most sensible option. 'I had terrible difficulty in contacting Mehmet and I had to take the entire stock to Istanbul with me,' she said quickly. 'I knew we wanted it here as soon as possible, so I've given it to a friend to bring home for me. He should be here in a few days.'

'Who?'

'No one you've met . . . He deals in carpets himself, so he'll know how to take care of them.'

'What's his name?' Melanie demanded suspiciously.
'Aram.'

'Sounds like some foreigner you met,' she commented disapprovingly. 'I don't remember you mentioning him before.'

Zelda found herself defending Aram in a way she'd never have thought possible less than a week ago. 'He's a perfectly respectable Englishman! There's absolutely nothing to worry about—he's due back here in a few days, and he's saved us the cost of transporting the carpets ourselves.'

'Did you give him everything you bought?' Rick looked appalled.

'Of course not,' she said scornfully, but if it was possible to blush inwardly, then that was what she was doing. She *had* given the bulk of carpets to Aram, and she had let him take the one rug on which they were likely to make a really big profit, to prove something to him that was just between the two of them.

In the light of her partners' reactions it did seem a little unwise to have let someone she had known just one week take anything—let alone contemplated giving him the whole stock. Yet that was exactly what she would have done if she hadn't had Rick and Melanie to answer to.

'I've got the most valuable ones with me—including these.' She spread out the carpets in front of them—luckily they were the two best. They might prove a distraction from the subject of Aram. 'Well, what do you think of them? Guess how much I paid for each one!'

Then, even Melanie was impressed.

The three of them spent a while speculating on profits. Zelda was gratified, but, as Rick pointed out to her, in the circumstances there wasn't much else for them to do.

The following days got progressively worse.

She was missing Aram more than she could ever have imagined possible. They had spent at least half their time together quarrelling, and she had been so very deter-

mined to fight him off at first, but, without quite
knowing how it had happened, she found that he had
become the centre of her life. Perhaps those last two
idyllic days in Istanbul had had a lot to do with it, giving
them an opportunity to explore the attraction they had
for each other without any of the earlier antagonism.
But that magical time was now beginning to seem like
some bright dream that had no substance in reality.

She had a wide circle of friends, some of whom she
hadn't seen for several months, but each time the phone
rang and there was yet another invitation for her, she
couldn't help indulging that sudden tingling sense of ex-
pectation that it just might be Aram—which was invariably followed by disappointment. At first, she
accepted the invitations, while she was certain that there
was little chance of contact from Turkey, but as time
wore on and the likelihood of hearing from Aram increased, she refused to go out in case she missed his call.
Instead, she found herself wandering aimlessly round her
flat, night after night, unable to concentrate on anything.

Meanwhile the debts were mounting up, and Zelda had
discovered a chilling reality for herself. Financially
speaking, you either went forwards or backwards—there
was no standing still. Not spending any money didn't
mean that the entries in the debits columns came to a
halt. And it didn't take the look of strain on Melanie's
face to tell her that if they couldn't get their hands on
some cash fast, they wouldn't be able to meet *any* of
their commitments, let alone keep the Magic Carpets
Company going. It seemed like the end of their
ambitions.

Considering the mess they were all in, it seemed selfish
to mind so much about her own private relationship with
Aram. So, as much to take her mind off his continuing
silence as anything, she did try to give some serious
thought as to whether or not one of her brothers might
actually be able to help them. But then pride intervened,
and she couldn't bring herself to ask. Anyway, Jem's

price would probably amount to ownership of the whole company, and neither she nor Rick nor Melanie would be able to call their lives their own again. Mike and George, in their own antiques business, might give her some sound advice but in exchange she'd have to put up with a lot of unwelcome patronage. And Dom would be useless—he didn't have any money, and her own ideas were just as good as his.

Eventually she decided to ring her father. He was a businessman, he had a sense of humour, and she could get what she wanted out of him when she had to. One more thing in his favour was that he never actually *said* 'I told you so', although she wouldn't put it past him one day to have the words emblazoned on his tie.

He offered to buy her lunch, which was a further plus factor, and, over a glass of wine of the kind she could only afford to drink if he was paying for it, she told him the story of the burglary.

'And so I suppose you want to borrow some money?' David Denton had grey eyes like his daughter's, and they showed humour in just the way hers did. He would have gone to the stake for his belief that he had no favourites among his children—he was equally strict with all his sons. It was just that he never remembered to include his daughter.

'Dad!' she exclaimed reproachfully. 'When was the last time I asked you for any money? I just want some advice.'

'You're in luck—advice is free today. I take it you don't want the tribe to hear anything about this?' His eyes twinkled at her through the wire-rimmed bifocals he wore. He had always understood her need to compete with her brothers, and, admiring her independence and spirit, had secretly aided and abetted her.

She couldn't be sure that news of the burglary hadn't filtered through already on one of the many possible grapevines, but joked half-heartedly about the way in which rumours could damage trade, and then, after a few astute questions, he offered the depressing opinion that short of a large and timely injection of cash from a bank loan or other source, unspecified, the present unhealthy condition of their trading company would prove to be terminal.

'Can I give you some money—or *lend* if you'd prefer?' he asked.

She met his eyes directly, and then pulled a rueful face. 'Thanks, Dad. I really appreciate that, but you understand why I can't say yes, don't you?'

He gave a wry smile. 'In your position, you know, none of your brothers would be so scrupulous. I could negotiate a loan for you through Alan Cartwright, if that'd be any help. But don't let the debts mount up or you'll be lucky to get clear of them.'

'Put like that, there's a lot to be said for bankruptcy,' she replied gloomily. 'Thanks again, Dad, but I still feel that making use of your personal tame bank manager is cheating a bit, and, anyway, we've already taken out as big a loan as we could risk—and that was in the days when we had something to sell! If only we could get our hands on the insurance money, but they're still quibbling about those wretched locks. They're objecting that the work we had done on them wasn't adequate. Still, we've got *some* hopeful prospects . . .'

She didn't add that the only hopeful prospect she had in mind just then was a dark-haired, hawk-nosed Franco-Polish-Armenian Englishman from whom she'd heard not one word, despite ardent promises, in well over a week. She wasn't sure that she could cope with the questions that would inevitably follow, and, viewed from her father's angle, she could understand how her story could look very different. The way he might see it, she had fallen in love with someone out of sheer relief that he hadn't turned out to be a terrorist, and then let herself be emotionally blackmailed into trusting him with most of her carpets!

But if her father guessed that there might be more to her unusually subdued manner than worry over the company, he wisely gave no hint of it. And, forced to look at the whole thing, however briefly, from another point of view, Zelda began to have creeping doubts. *Why* hadn't Aram rung her? He had told her it might be difficult for the first week, but after that surely he could have found his way to a phone?

On analysis, she realised that most of her doubts centred round the fact that he hadn't been able to tell her what she most desperately wanted to hear—and then had to remind herself that he could have said he loved her just to please her, and it wouldn't have meant a thing. Or even worse—he might have said it believing he meant it, like Daniel. If she loved him, she should trust him. But she'd already found out in Turkey, over the question of the carpets, just how fragile a thing her own trust was. She still wasn't sure to what extent her arguments about protecting her partners' rights had been a blind for her own insecurity. That was something Aram might have seen more clearly than she. If she really trusted him—really loved him—then the question of risk shouldn't have arisen.

By the beginning of the third week, bankruptcy was looking like quite a sound proposition from everyone's point of view except Zelda's. They had tried to keep the warehouse open, in the hopes that a prospective customer might ring, or drop in to see what they'd got. She and Rick had taken it in turns to answer the restored phone and guard the few carpets that they now ferried back to Melanie's every evening. They'd had several interested enquiries, but they hadn't sold anything. And every time someone had passed the warehouse doors during one of her turns to 'mind the shop', Zelda had looked up, filled with the unreasonable hope that somehow it would be Aram. Of course it never was, and, although the sense of disappointment each time was just as keen, underneath a fear began to grow that Rick's

initial horror at her entrusting the carpets to someone
she'd only just met might prove to be well founded. Aram
didn't love her, she knew that. In business terms, he was
a sort of rival. It was true he seemed to deal in a quality
of merchandise she couldn't afford to buy, but her own
rugs were valuable too... Supposing he *wasn't* honest?
She didn't want to let herself think that way, but it was
becoming increasingly difficult to quell the doubts.

Then Melanie dropped a bombshell.

'Somebody's made an offer for us!' she announced
on Friday morning, as Zelda arrived on her doorstep, it
being her turn to fetch the carpets and mind the shop.
'Somebody actually thinks we're a good thing, debts and
all!'

Zelda was stunned. It took her several seconds to
adjust her thoughts. 'They must be out of their skulls!
When did you hear?'

'Just last night, after you'd gone. I had a phone call
from a dealer's. I told them we'd had a burglary, but
there was more of our stock "in transit". The chap I
spoke to—Charles someone—I can't remember—I wrote
it down—said the burglary might not make a difference.
He said he'd get his own solicitor on to the problem with
the insurance, but it was the company itself they were
interested in—which means *us*! We've just been head-
hunted!'

'But if somebody else buys us, we won't be independent any more. We'll have to do everything the way
they want it!' Zelda protested. 'If only we could hang
on just a bit longer—with the insurance money and the
stuff I got in Turkey this time I'm sure we could make
up everything we've lost.'

'We won't be very independent if we wind up in prison
for debt,' her partner pointed out sharply. 'And where
are the rest of your carpets? Have you heard anything
from your Aram friend?'

Zelda shook her head and changed the subject. If the
take-over could go ahead, stock or no stock, it wouldn't

really matter to them in the long run if a shady dealer called Kalinsky had made off into the blue with the rest of their carpets. It wouldn't matter to the company, that was. She didn't want to have to face the thought just now of what it might to do her personally. 'What's the name of this loony dealer's that wants to buy us?' The question was as much to distract herself as Melanie.

'Marten and Palmer. I've definitely heard of them.'

'So have I. They're not in the least the sort of people who'd be interested in us. What do you think's going on?' The name was somehow familiar in a recent context, but she couldn't immediately recall when or where she'd heard it.

Melanie shrugged. 'I don't think I really care, the whole thing's such a relief. I've been doing some sums, and even if the insurance came through tomorrow we'd still have a terrible struggle ahead of us. We weren't really winning before the burglary—not fast enough, anyway. This is like a gift from the gods as far as I'm concerned.'

They didn't discuss it further then, but Zelda was left with plenty of food for thought.

And the more she thought, the more she was convinced that Marten and Palmer was the firm Aram had told her he had recently taken over, in which case, why weren't they calling themselves Kalinsky's? And who was this Charles person who had contacted Melanie? Was he for some reason acting independently, or was Aram himself behind the bid? Always assuming, of course, he had told her the truth about the take-over... He could have concocted the whole story to make himself sound more respectable, and to make her more inclined to entrust him with her carpets... But before she let her doubts run away with her she *had* to know whether Aram was behind the offer for her company.

They were three days into the fourth week since her return from Turkey, when she succeeded in contacting the elusive 'Charles'. He turned out to be Charles Palmer, a nephew of one of the original owners. He had apparently been out of town on business, but his matter-of-fact replies to Zelda's questions on the link with Kalinsky's at first filled her with relief, making her darker suspicions of Aram seem very silly.

In his low, quiet voice Charles said that yes, the firm was now Kalinsky's, but was going to continue to trade for a while under the old name. Yes, Aram Kalinsky was behind the offer for Magic Carpets—he had phoned them from Istanbul over three weeks ago to give them instructions, but no, he hadn't contacted them since. He, Charles, had proceeded as far as he could in Mr Kalinsky's absence, but he was hoping to set up a meeting with Zelda and her partners to discuss the situation further, so that when Mr Kalinsky came back they would be in a position to finalise the deal.

Zelda was in a turmoil, but, most ridiculously, her strongest feeling was one of elation—her dark-haired enigmatic carpet dealer wasn't just a figment of her own imagination: Aram *did* exist—quite independently of her—and respectable businessmen knew all about him! And that meant that he hadn't just disappeared with her carpets, and more important still—everything that had happened in Istanbul was real too...

'But does he know about the burglary?' she protested, trying to hang on to the facts that had nothing to do with her private feelings for him. 'Surely that's changed the situation?'

'I was under the impression that Mr Kalinsky was keen to acquire the company no matter what the condition of its finances, and Miss Sharman told me you were fully insured.'

Charles Palmer sounded very nice, and from the company point of view what he had to tell her looked like good news. But something in what he had just said introduced a faint thread of doubt.

'When exactly did Ar—Mr Kalinsky——' she corrected herself hastily '—first find out about us? All this seems a bit sudden.' Surely he couldn't have been going simply on what she had told him since their meeting in Turkey?

'Oh, he's been interested for some time. He's in Turkey at the moment, but he looked into the possibility of making an offer for you some weeks before he left.'

Some weeks before he left... Suddenly it was as though all the blood had drained away from her heart. Her hands were cold, and, although she was staring at the telephone in front of her, her eyes didn't seem to be focused... He must have known who she was from the beginning! He had kept his investigations into the company very discreet—neither she nor Rick nor Melanie had had the slightest idea anyone was interested in them—but he must have found out enough about her to have identified her very quickly from those early conversations in the Syrian desert. And that meant that all the bargaining over her carpet, all the challenges and the bets could no longer be taken as the joke he had pretended. He'd been using her to find out more about the company. She remembered how many questions he'd asked, and how few he'd answered, keeping his own interests a secret. He must have been amused that his name had given away nothing to her, and deliberately taken advantage of her ignorance.

Her mind seemed to be working independently of her will, putting together the final pieces of the mysterious pattern she no longer wanted to see. The key to it had always been Aram, and she had longed to discover what lay behind the enigma. Well, now she knew.

The hopes that the mere confirmation of his existence had revived in her died instantly. He'd been using her all along... And if he'd really cared about her, knowing how much it meant to her, he'd have respected her independence. She remembered now that curious conversation they'd had in Istanbul—all along she'd known there was something behind it. How stupid she'd been not to see what he was driving at.

The sense of betrayal was so acute it was a genuine physical pain. Her throat ached as though she'd swallowed a knife, and she didn't even stop to think what she was saying. Aram—making a complete fool of her in the process—had succeeded in hurting her more than she had thought possible, and her instinct was to try to hurt back. She was going to stop him taking over the company if it was the last thing she did.

'Your Mr Kalinsky must be out of his mind!' she choked, ignoring the pang that told her it wasn't fair to take this out on a stranger at the other end of the line— a mere business associate could have nothing to do with the personal concerns of the man who had so cold-bloodedly involved her in a love-affair, exploiting her vulnerability for his own ends.

'No one buys a company like ours—with nothing but a lot of debts! And haven't you forgotten something? We might not *all* want to sell!'

And with that she slammed down the receiver.

Although her parting shot to Charles had been delivered with all the conviction of an emotion that was threatening to overwhelm her, even as she said it she knew that unless she won Melanie over to her side it was no more than an empty threat. Rick would support his cousin no matter what, and she would be powerless against the two of them.

In an attempt to keep at bay the thought of Aram's betrayal—the way he had used her—she packed up for the afternoon at the warehouse, and went straight to Melanie's.

The pain in her heart made her more aggressive than she had ever been as she swept into Melanie's 'office', her eyes blazing with unshed tears. All the way there she had been desperately persuading herself that it would be the final humiliation to cry over someone so obviously worthless.

'You realise that this Mr Kalinsky who's behind the offer and the Aram person who has my carpets are one and the same, don't you?' she challenged instantly.

Melanie stared at her in undisguised astonishment, and then shrugged. 'So? Surely that's good news. What's got into you? At least it means he'll bring the rest of the carpets back—even if they *are* his by the time he gets here.'

'That's just what I want to talk to you about,' Zelda said bitterly. 'This isn't the straightforward little miracle it appears. I've found out from Charles that Aram knew who I was all the time we were together in Turkey and he was just using me to get more information about the company. He knows perfectly well how important it is for us to be independent, and this is his way of showing he doesn't give a damn!'

Melanie continued to stare at her. 'Don't be ridiculous, Zel. We've got no choice about being independent any longer—you know that. So what if he was checking us out? You must have given Magic Carpets one hell of a press, because it's *us* he really wants—Charles told me. That's why our finances—given a bit of extra cash, which we personally don't have, and a bit of time which we also don't have—aren't any real concern to him. He's a businessman—you make it sound as though he's trying to make some sort of personal score in this.'

'He is!' Zelda admitted miserably. 'He wants our company—yes—but it's all part of a game to him. He had a bet with me over a carpet I bought. I wouldn't sell it to him even at a four hundred per cent profit, and this is his way of acquiring it!'

Melanie looked sceptical. 'Where's the carpet now?'

'He's got it.'

'So why doesn't he just hang on to it? You're not making sense. No one takes over a tin-pot little company like ours for *one* carpet! And haven't you forgotten something? If he knew who you were before he made the bet, then he was interested in the company from the start. Some game he was playing with you over one carpet wasn't going to make any difference. What's got into you, Zel? It's not like you to be so illogical.'

Now that first passionate fury of her rejection of Aram was beginning to fade under Melanie's cool glance, Zelda could see very clearly that what she was going to ask was impossible. She cleared her throat painfully. 'It's not as simple as that ... It wasn't only the bet about the carpet—there was another one ...' Put like that, it was going to sound awful. 'I thought it was just a joke at first ...'

'So what was it?' Melanie prompted curiously.

'That we ... that he'd have me.'

The cautious silence that met her bald statement hinted that her friend was beginning to understand the background to the unexpected outburst, and Zelda turned aside quickly, hastily brushing her cheeks with the back of her hand. She would find it only too easy to cry now if she let herself.

'Oh,' said Melanie, with obvious sympathy. 'Then that puts a different aspect on the whole thing from your point of view, I can see that. But, Zel, I can't afford to antagonise him over the offer. We've still got to let him buy us out.'

'Over my dead body!' Defiance was one way at least to avoid giving in to those tears, but it lacked any real conviction. She was opposing some very personal, very mixed-up wishes against the greater good of the company. Instead, she would have to come to her own private decision over what she was going to do about Aram.

But to her surprise Melanie looked as though she too was on the verge of giving in to the temptation to weep.

'We *have* to sell,' she pleaded. 'Don't let your personal feelings, whatever they may be, cloud your judgement over this! There's no way I can get us out of the mess we're in now. I don't have the experience, and quite honestly I don't think I've got the determination any more... I'm tired of fighting. I want someone else to take over the responsibilities for a while—someone else to stay awake at night worrying.' She hesitated for a second, and then went on more calmly. 'It's a dream of a deal. He's going to give us the freedom to make our own decisions, and go on running Magic Carpets very much as we want while he takes a lot of the financial worries off our backs.'

Zelda couldn't trust herself to speak—she'd think about the implications of that later.

Melanie was looking at her consideringly. Then she said slowly, 'After what you've just told me, I'd guess that you're the one behind it. He wants you, Zel—you're our best asset. Rick and I only come along with the package deal.'

'That's not true and you know it—we're a team,' Zelda protested loyally. 'But he definitely wants to get the better of me...' Her tone was bitter again. 'I suppose, about the take-over, Rick agrees with you?'

Melanie nodded. 'I talked to him again late last night. He thinks it's the only way out. We can't go on increasing the debts. If we take out another loan—assuming anyone will give us one—to tide us over until the insurance pay up, we'll be paying even more interest on that. We'll never make ends meet.'

It was the message she'd got from her talk with her father. Looking at Melanie now, she could see the toll the last couple of weeks had taken. Her friend looked as though she literally hadn't slept for days. And it was true, she was the one who had had to shoulder all the responsibilities while Zelda herself had been swanning off to far-away places, enjoying the added zest that having to keep within a tight budget had added to the cut and thrust of bargaining. But tight budgets hadn't been much fun in London—Melanie must have been nearly out of her mind with worry the last few weeks, even though in her usual calm rather offhand manner she had given little sign of it.

Torn between her confused feelings about Aram and concern for her friend, Zelda slipped an arm round Melanie's shoulders. 'I'm sorry, I know I'm being selfish,' she said at last with difficulty. 'You've had a far worse time of it than me and I won't be against you over the offer from Kalinsky's. I just wish it had been somebody else.'

Melanie sighed. 'Thanks, Zel. I knew you'd see sense. I have to confess it'll be a great relief to have people to turn to who really know what they're doing.'

There was a pause, and then she asked tentatively, 'I'll understand if you don't want to talk about it...but what *did* go on between you and this mysterious Mr Kalinsky?'

Zelda swallowed. Now that that first furious resentment had drained away she was too perilously close to tears.

'It—it's not easy to explain...'

'Are you in love with him?'

'Yes.' It was still true, otherwise it wouldn't hurt so much.

'Is he in love with you?'

'No.' It hurt even more now to admit that, out loud. Once spoken, it seemed to put the matter beyond any doubt.

Melanie looked at her thoughtfully. 'You sound very certain.'

'He told me.' It was hard just to get the words out. She forced herself to go on. 'All the time I think he was...just trying to prove a point. Like the point about the carpet.'

'But he wants you working for him!' her friend objected. And then, even as Melanie spoke, Zelda found she had come to a decision. She realised suddenly that in her impetuous bid to get Melanie to oppose the deal, it was this she had really been working towards without knowing it.

She wasn't going to discuss it, with Melanie or anyone—but she wasn't going to work for Aram. Ever.

She couldn't oppose the Kalinsky offer effectively on personal grounds—she'd known that from the start, and now it wouldn't be fair to Melanie—but she didn't have to work for Aram once the deal had gone through. And, when that was finalised, she was going to be out of the company and its director's life so fast he wouldn't even have time to blink.

Her decision didn't make her feel any better. The future still looked bleak.

Once she had agreed not to oppose the deal, Zelda expected everything to happen quickly. But then she was forced to admit that her part in the negotiations had been relatively insignificant. They were all waiting for Aram to show up.

The obvious conclusion to draw from his silence towards herself was that he had got exactly what he wanted: her in bed, and the company—which included the carpet. He had made good his boast, cleverly using that latent attraction between them to tie her up in emotional knots. And it had been oh, so clever! He had never even had to tell her a lie, refusing to commit himself about his feelings towards her, and withholding the information which would have allowed her to see his actions in their true perspective. And, in the process, he had gained his petty revenge for the way she had got the better of him when they had first met—and now that he hadn't seen her for a while, he had lost interest in her. True, he didn't appear to have contacted Charles either, but then he probably didn't think he needed to; he'd given him his instructions over three weeks ago from Istanbul.

It was she who had begun to lie, persuading herself that it was only a matter of time before he realised the true nature of his feelings for her. But time had passed, and he obviously felt no differently. She didn't want to have to see him ever again, and to protect herself against some of the hurt she tried hard to believe that she hated

him. But all the time, underneath, she knew she had
done the one thing she had promised herself would never
happen again—she had given her heart to someone who
didn't really want it. This time it was so much worse
than before. She knew if she let herself dwell on it she
would start to cry, and if she started to cry she would
never stop...

The beginning of the following week, Charles rang to
confirm the final meeting before the signing of the contract, and also to confirm what Zelda already half hoped
for, half feared: Aram was due back in London that
morning, and was anxious to get the whole thing settled.
They would all meet at the Kalinsky offices the next
day—and that *all* provoked a good deal of discussion.

She had made up her mind the instant she heard that
Aram was due back. She would take herself off immediately and indefinitely to stay with Dominic, swearing
Melanie and Rick to secrecy first. Since he hadn't even
attempted to explain his long absence, or four week
silence, she wanted to make sure there was no chance of
seeing him now. She no longer wanted to hear any explanations—she was hurting far too much to listen to
any bland businessman's excuses. Her letter of resig-
nation, which he would have on his desk the morning
after he acquired Magic Carpets, was all she had to say
to him. She refused to attend the meeting.

As far as Rick and Melanie were concerned, that didn't
matter. Nobody else seemed to object either—except
Aram. He had rung Melanie from Charles's office demanding to speak to Zelda, who had at that moment
been transferring some of her things to Dominic's flat,
prior to establishing her secret retreat. There was a
message that she was to ring him back, and a string of
numbers at which he could be reached.

On being presented with the list, Zelda felt her heart
constrict painfully. 'Business, I suppose?' she managed
offhandedly, in a desperate attempt to hide how much

the answer mattered to her. 'Did he say why he didn't send me so much as a postcard?'

'I don't think so.' Melanie's reply was vague, but she gave her friend a shrewd look. 'He's got such a sexy voice I wasn't really listening to what he said—oh, except he wants to know why you're never at home to answer the phone and why you won't attend the meeting. And something about a goat.'

'Huh.' She tried to sound flippant. 'Probably some skin rug he'd cheated someone out of. There's not much to choose between Aram Kalinsky and the average brigand. I'm not going, and that's flat.'

She threw away the sheet of paper Melanie had given her and went straight back to Dominic's. But in the end she hadn't had any choice about the meeting. Aram insisted he wanted all the partners in Magic Carpets Company present and without her it wouldn't take place.

It was an occasion that was going to be overawingly formal. But somehow in the context of the West End offices of Marten and Palmer—now Kalinsky's—the efforts made by the Magic Carpets Company to look respectable weren't quite up to the mark. Melanie was wearing a business suit and some make-up, but her hair wasn't much better, and Rick, in his guise of artistic trendy, had a loose-jacketed suit too but was tie-less. Only Zelda, although she was dressed like Melanie, wasn't trying to make a good impression on anyone, she told herself rather desperately. In these formal business surroundings it was an attempt at camouflage. She was only going along because she had to, and intended to take as little part in the proceedings as she could. Afterwards she would escape back to Dominic's before the ink was dry on the contract.

Kalinsky's offices were undeniably smart—no shelf supports drilled into unplastered brick here, or telephone somewhere on the floor because the scratched old second-hand desk was piled high with papers that wouldn't fit into a battered filing cabinet. Even the

Kalinsky plants had had their leaves polished by a contractor who came in specially for the purpose.

The managing director's office—Aram's, to be precise—had a carpet that felt six inches thick, and leather furniture so large that even two armchairs, if transferred to the warehouse, would have seriously reduced valuable storage space in the days when they'd had some stock to store. There were original pictures on the walls that looked as though they were expensive...in fact everything was individual and expensive, as though someone's personal taste had dictated quite a lot about this office.

Zelda spent a great deal of time looking at the décor. She had deliberately come in last, behind Rick despite his attempts to be polite. Now she placed herself behind Rick and Melanie, vaguely aware of the mild middle-aged Charles standing somewhere behind her. Because somewhere in front, where she didn't want to look, was Aram. There were polite greetings going on, and the second he spoke her ear picked out those deep, slightly rough tones that sent a little shiver down her spine.

Everyone was shaking hands. Then Aram was taking her belatedly outstretched hand in his and she was avoiding looking at him. But his touch was instantly familiar, and his fingers suddenly held hers tightly. Startled, she met his eyes for one instant and it seemed as though he was going to kiss her but because it would no longer mean anything she stepped back before she could betray herself. Then he let go of her hand. She was trembling so much she thought everyone must be able to see.

There were too many complicated feelings fighting in her at once—misery, that what she had most hoped might happen between them had never really been a possibility, except in her mind; resentment that he had used her, coupled with the painful irony of the way in which he had finally made good his boast about the carpet;

and a new feeling she couldn't come to terms with: a sense of overwhelming humiliation.

So unfamiliar in his expensive suit and silk shirt and fashion-house tie, Aram was as much a stranger to her now as that first time she had seen him—a whole lifetime ago—standing in a dusty little clutter of houses out in the Syrian desert. It had the effect of distancing her suddenly from everything, and she wondered what this new stranger could possibly think of the people who had just walked into his office. She had boasted of Melanie and Rick and herself—the Magic Carpets Company that was really going places. It all sounded so childish now. The warehouse with its brick walls and draughts and spiders was a world away from this office.

And, just like children, they had got themselves into trouble in a risky world they didn't understand, and they needed his help to get them out of it. But now that he must discover from its shabby representatives what the Magic Carpets Company was really about, perhaps he wouldn't want anything more to do with them ...

She wondered if she could say anything to bring this awful interview to a close, before Melanie and Rick could realise their humiliation too, and that it was partly her fault they were in this false situation—but they were chatting easily with Charles Palmer, and another man whose name she hadn't listened to, and she was aware of the deep edgy voice from time to time and she knew he was looking at her.

'What do you think, Zelda?'

She stared at Melanie in horror. What had she asked her?

The others laughed. And then Rick said, 'She's been examining your carpet—Zelda's our whiz-kid carpet buyer. She probably doesn't think much of your Wilton.'

He had turned it into a joke and she felt intensely grateful to him. At that moment her most passionate wish had been that the carpet, the floor below it, and the floors below that, might suddenly open like the proverbial earth and mercifully swallow her.

She saw Aram smiling at her, and wondered what he was thinking. His smile went right through her, turning her bones to water, and she stood there, hating him for setting her up like this, and just because, by looking at her, he could still make her want him.

Then Charles said, 'Zelda's one of your biggest assets—and I have that on the best authority.'

'Melanie's?' she asked quickly, trying to recover.

Charles laughed. 'No, Aram's. He's seen you in action.'

There was no deliberate ambiguity in the words, but Zelda instantly wondered if Aram with his characteristic irony wasn't applying them in a completely different context. She looked desperately at Melanie to rescue her from the renewed confusion that suddenly came over her. Her awareness of Aram was making her behave like an idiot and she resented that.

Then Aram said, 'I hear you're not wholly in favour of this deal, Zelda. Why is that exactly?' It was a direct challenge. He hadn't missed how little she had contributed to the discussion.

'You know why!' she said, summoning up some of her old defiance. 'And if you don't, you can guess.'

He raised one dark eyebrow, registering surprise, but said nothing. She caught sight of Charles and the other man shifting uneasily, and Melanie and Rick looked at each other.

They sat down, sinking into those luxurious chairs as though they were going to lounge away the whole morning, and the terms of the agreement were discussed generally. Officially, Melanie and Charles had already thrashed out all the points for negotiation.

Zelda remained silent, knowing that Melanie, who was fully aware of her unwillingness to be there, would talk for her. She stared at the floor, unable to shut out those deep edgy tones no matter how hard she tried not to listen, and wished herself a thousand miles away.

Then she heard Aram say, 'I think that just about sews it up, don't you? Charles? Oliver?'

Oliver, of course. Marten's solicitor. She tried to fix her mind on anything that wasn't Aram. She hadn't known until now that it was possible for unhappiness to cause such intense physical pain.

Then there was a general signing of papers, and some desultory conversation which didn't involve her. All she was aware of was a silence that seemed to fill the whole room, even though it was only between herself and the tall dark-haired man standing behind the mahogany desk.

She would go now. She'd send her excuses about the lunch afterwards. Escape was vital.

'Perhaps we could all head towards the restaurant for a pre-celebratory-lunch drink?' Charles suggested. 'While you were *enjoying yourself* so much in Turkey, some people were doing the work round here. I for one could do with a bit of relaxation—preferably alcoholic.'

The heavy emphasis on some of Charles's words caught her attention—had Aram told him of his brief affair with her? That was just another twist of the knife.

She saw Aram give him that familiar grin. His tan was several shades darker than Zelda's, and against the London pallor of the others just for a second he looked every bit the hawk-nosed predator she had first thought him, all those weeks ago. Another lifetime.

'That's fine,' he said slowly. 'You go on ahead. Start without us if necessary...'

Us?

'I want to talk to Zelda alone.'

CHAPTER NINE

ARAM'S tone didn't invite further discussion. Zelda saw Melanie give her a quick, helpless look before she was ushered out by Charles and Oliver, Rick beside her. There were acres of empty space where they had been, and a closed door that shut off their voices.

Then there was silence.

Zelda felt her mouth go dry, and it was as though there were butterflies trapped in all her veins, fluttering desperately to escape. Aram was looking at her, but he wasn't smiling.

Finally, to break the silence, she said foolishly, her voice treacherously uneven, 'So this is the other part of your bet—that you'd have the Turkish carpet in the end... Wouldn't it have been simpler just to steal it?'

'Maybe.' He seemed suddenly remote, almost cold, a long way from the man she had known in Istanbul. He hadn't made a move towards her, and remained standing casually propped against the desk, arms folded, watching her. Like some bank manager, she thought, meeting a customer for the first time and assessing them as a bad risk. The smart offices, the expensively dressed managing director—they were all such a long way from the cheerful backstreet bargaining that she understood...

Then, with so many things wrong between them, it was that sense of humiliation she had experienced earlier that swept over her first, and she couldn't bear it. 'I didn't ask you to buy us, Aram!' she burst out. 'You shouldn't have believed everything I said when we were in Turkey!'

A quick frown crossed that hawk-like face. 'What exactly was it that I shouldn't have believed?' His voice sounded harsh, and although he had hardly moved a muscle she found him newly intimidating.

'The company—the carpets—everything!'

Again there was that keen look, and she remembered how the first time she had seen him she had thought that the colour of his eyes was the curious green-blue of old bottle glass. Now their expression was as cold and as hard. She remembered how he had been wearing the eye-patch, and how unscrupulous it had made him look. Dressing in a smart businessman's suit didn't make him appear any the less predatory now; if anything, he seemed even more of a threat, as though the brigand had been given a veneer of civilisation that made him even more dangerous.

She opened her mouth to say something more to fill that awful silence again, and then realised that what she had just said could have been interpreted in a way she had never meant. In the context of their relationship, that 'everything' could amount to a denial of all she had ever felt for him.

But there was no point trying to explain now. In Istanbul he had told her it was too soon to be sure of his feelings. He had asked her to wait—but what was there to wait for? Now, so unexpectedly faced with this cold, clever businessman, she knew all the rest had just been a dream.

'What did you want to say to me, Aram?' She lifted her chin a little in defiance, and blinked rapidly to hide any suspicious glitter in her eyes. 'Because if this is just a social chat, I've got more pressing things to do—like finding a new job.'

She hadn't meant to say that: it was a parting shot she had been saving up for tomorrow, but, as always, her emotions got the better of her suddenly—and it did provoke a reaction.

That steely length of him seemed to uncoil itself like a spring, and he was standing over her before she had a chance to step back. Roughly, he took hold of her chin, forcing her to meet his gaze.

'Oh, no, you don't,' he said softly, almost as though it were a threat. 'You're part of the company I've bought—a very vital part—you're working for me!'

'And what if I don't want to?' she flung at him. 'You can't make me!'

Disconcertingly green eyes narrowed, and that well-shaped mouth turned down a little at the corners. 'No,' he said slowly, 'I wouldn't choose to say I could *make* you do anything—but I could persuade you...'

He was studying her face as attentively as though he were about to draw or paint it. Then he was looking at her mouth, and that terrible weakness swept through her like fire and his touch seemed to burn her. The anger and resentment she had been building up so carefully against just such a meeting as this seemed to have melted away in an instant, as though it had never been. Oh, my darling, make it all right! she was begging silently. Just kiss me, tell me you love me—I can't bear this! She longed for him to take her in his arms.

And then she knew that although she hadn't allowed for just how powerfully his very nearness could affect her, *he* surely had. He must sense that he had only to touch her and he could do anything with her—something he must have discovered the very first time he had really kissed her, during that rainstorm at Göreme. The realisation humiliated her—and suddenly she understood something else. Merely telling her he loved her—not that he would, of course—wasn't enough any longer. It would never be enough, because, without any real commitment on his side, he would be able to manipulate her just like this, and she would always be vulnerable, always insecure. No one but a fool would resume an affair on those terms. So... this really had to be the end.

She turned her face away from him, stepping back out of his reach. 'What have you done with my carpets?' she asked unsteadily. 'You took long enough getting back with them—or have you sold them already?' She tried to sound sarcastic to hide the feelings that were threatening to overwhelm her.

'They're my carpets now, Zelda!' His voice told her that he was smiling, and in just the way she didn't like. 'But there's something we haven't cleared up yet. Why exactly were you so relucant to come to this meeting? I've been ringing you since late last night—where the hell were you?'

Of course, it was the meeting he was concerned about. The take-over. How silly of her to have hoped, even for one fleeting moment, that he might be about to say something about missing her...

'Staying with my brother,' she said reluctantly. 'But, since we've got to the subject of phone calls, weren't you supposed to ring me three weeks ago? Didn't it occur to you that I might wonder where you'd got to with all my carpets?'

She walked across to the window, and stood with her back turned to him gazing down into the street. It hurt too much to think about the nights waiting for those phone calls. Instead she concentrated desperately on the smart office blocks outside the window, and the fine old buildings. And they didn't even have a skylight at the warehouse...

'Didn't you know I hadn't contacted Charles either?'

'Yes, I heard,' she said.

'And...?' he prompted. 'What conclusion did you come to?'

'I thought perhaps you didn't need to, because I also heard something else.' It was amazing how cool her own voice sounded in her ears when everything inside her seemed to be tying itself into agonised knots.

Then there was a long silence, until he said from somewhere behind her, 'And what exactly was that?'

She took a very deep breath. 'You'd been looking into our company before we even met in Syria.'

'Yes?' He sounded puzzled. 'What's wrong with that?'

'So you knew who I was?'

'Yes,' he said again. 'You were pointed out to me at an auction in London some months ago—just about the time when I first heard of Magic Carpets. I thought you looked familiar when I saw you with that Syrian, and when I started to talk to you I was sure. Then I couldn't resist the opportunity to get to know you better. Zelda— what's all this about?'

Ignoring his question, she turned quickly to face him, her eyes accusing. 'So you used me to find out about the company!'

He had moved closer, standing now only a few feet away, still watching her. Then she saw his eyes narrow slightly, and that familiar hateful sarcasm was in his voice. 'Aren't we a little over-emotive in our choice of word there? Not *used*, Zelda. You told me nothing about the company I didn't know already. But I will admit that at first I was testing you. I was curious to see how good you really were.'

He sounded so cold, so detached that she reacted instantly. It all made sense now—all that ridiculous bargaining, all those questions. 'And I suppose since we've been honoured by a take-over I must have passed with flying colours?' This time her tone matched his, but she didn't wait for a reply. 'And I suppose all those things I told you about wanting our independence and how important it was to succeed on our own didn't mean anything to you once I'd confirmed what you wanted to know about the company? I was stupid to believe you even *listened*!'

The sarcasm suddenly came to a choked halt when she knew she was going to cry if she said any more.

There was a brief pause and then he asked slowly, 'Why don't you trust me—you don't, do you?'

'No.' She avoided his gaze. He made her feel too vulnerable.

'Then why did you let me take the carpets? Zelda, *look* at me!'

'I didn't have much of an alternative.' She wasn't going to look him in the eye. It wasn't trust they had been talking about in Istanbul—it was love. But there was no point in admitting any of her feelings now, and her pride wouldn't let him get anything out of her.

'Yes, you did.' His reply was blunt, admitting no argument. 'You could have put them all on the plane—you could have arranged for your Turkish friend to have them picked up—I refuse to believe that someone as resourceful as you would have been at a loss having got them that far. So you chose to trust me. Why are you denying it now?'

'All right! I admit—I chose to trust you ... *then*.'

'So what's happened since to change it?'

He was making her feel trapped. There were tears of frustration pricking behind her eyes. She couldn't tell him the real reason. That was a discussion they'd already had, over four weeks ago in Istanbul. He'd given her his answer then, and he clearly had nothing to add to it she wanted to hear.

'Oh, I don't know——' she said desperately. 'Stop trying to cross-question me all the time! It's the bid for Magic Carpets...the fact that you said what you wanted and now you've got it ... everything!'

'At least your partners recognise a good thing when they see it,' he said bitterly. 'I notice Melanie's not complaining about losing her independence.'

'And that's another thing—you don't even know what you're buying!' She was all but shouting at him now, and if he came any closer she'd scream.

'All right,' he said slowly, 'so why don't you show me?'

So instead of the quick escape she had wanted, she found herself walking down with him to the powerful sports car that was parked in a nearby street, and then directing him through the traffic to the narrow lanes that led to the mews and the warehouse.

She gave one furtive glance at his profile, but he looked remote and forbidding. He hadn't argued with her, or tried to touch her again, but somehow she'd let herself be intimidated by that untested power he always seemed to hold in reserve. What was to follow might well prove to be even worse than the last half-hour spent in his company.

'It's grotty,' she said defensively, as the Porsche negotiated the last of the alleys. She felt almost sick with apprehension. All that wonderful romance in Turkey, all those intense hopes for the future had now finally boiled down to this—the moment when he would see the silly boast she had made in a childish attempt to get the better of him for what it was. 'It has one light bulb which is about the only thing the burglars left apart from the furniture. You'll tear up the contract when you see it. I warn you you've just been wasting your time.'

'And you've just been wasting your breath. Shut up.'

She winced inwardly at the sarcasm, and stared at her hands in her lap. She should have been used to that sort of reply by now.

She thought about her decision to find another job. Nothing he had said had caused her in any way to change her mind. If they'd only just met, if it were nothing but a business arrangement as it would be for the others, she wouldn't be opposing it so strongly, and selling out to Kalinsky's would have been a completely different matter. But now, in the circumstances, it would be sheer agony.

To be near him, to see him sometimes, maybe even to go to Turkey buying with him ... it would be impossible now that he could be no more to her than her employer. Because she wouldn't resume the affair. And that altered everything.

He was waiting for her to get out.

She wasn't used to wearing high heels, and she almost overbalanced on the cobblestones as she walked from the car.

'You look very glamorous,' he said, eyeing her from the other side of the bonnet. She was glad there was that distance between them. 'I've never seen you in a skirt. Not quite the Zelda I know—in more ways than one.'

She wasn't sure what he meant by that—but she wasn't going to ask.

She fitted the key into the new padlock and jiggled it. They'd changed all the locks again after the burglary—

rather pointlessly by then, as Rick had commented at the time. The lock was very stiff.

She was acutely conscious of Aram's hands on hers—the strong fingers curling round her own—as he reached across to turn the key.

'Let me.'

She withdrew her hands and stepped aside quickly when his arm brushed hers, letting him remove the padlock from the hasp and push the door open. It was dark inside, as always, but unusually empty, with that sad bereft look it had had since the burglary.

She switched on the light, and the solitary bulb hung uncompromisingly from its cord. She thought of the wall lights and plush carpets at Kalinsky's. And she thought again how this rich tycoon in his Savile Row suit had been someone she had imagined she initially despised because she could drive a harder bargain than he could, and now he had made a complete fool of her.

He was looking round, and the silence was so oppressive that she had to speak—to fill somehow the void of unspoken criticism that was all round her.

'The floor's uneven and damp comes up through the bricks, and the roof leaks and we've only got one telephone line. And the company only owns half of the van—the other half is Rick's—and there are no carpets here any more in case we get burgled again so Melanie's got them at home and——'

'Zelda,' he said quietly. 'Shut up.'

She had been talking to fill the silence—and to cover her own embarrassment brought face to face with a reality she had dressed in such flattering terms. The bricks looked dirtier and the ceiling more cobwebby than she had ever seen them.

She stared at the floor, and she knew that he was staring at her.

'What's the matter?' he asked then. 'You really didn't want me to buy the company?'

She shook her head. 'For Melanie and Rick, yes, if you mean what you say...'

'What do you mean, "if I mean what I say"?' That rough voice was edged with anger, and he took a step nearer, his height dominating her. 'Of course I bloody well mean what I say—I've just signed a contract to prove it! What do you think I am—some sort of city shark? Look at this place, Zelda——'

'I am looking!' she choked furiously, her grey eyes suspiciously bright. 'Don't think I don't know what *you* think—what you've been thinking all along! Charles must have told you what this was like and you've been enjoying making me look a fool ever since! I know that a company like Kalinsky's with everything going for it couldn't seriously be interested in people like us. What did we have to offer but a lot of debts? So now you've got your revenge from Turkey why don't you just take my Turkish carpet and leave it at that? I know you think this is just a Mickey Mouse outfit...' She tailed off. She would cry if she said any more.

He studied her in silence for a moment, then he said slowly, 'So that's what it's all about... I was wondering why none of it seemed to add up... But you've got it wrong.' His mouth quirked in a wry smile. 'You can't think much of me as a businessman if you believe I'd go to these lengths just to get the better of you over a silly game. Because that's all it was, Zelda. Just a game.'

Two things I'm going to promise you:...I'm going to have that carpet of yours in the end and—I'm going to have *you*! She could hear the words as clearly as if he'd just said them. She *had* to know. For the record if nothing else.

'Are we—are we just talking about the carpet?'

For a moment he looked puzzled. 'Of course. What else? So do you want to know what I really think about your "Mickey Mouse" company? I think you're all bloody marvellous.'

Suddenly, it was just as though he were talking in a foreign language. She wasn't sure she'd understood anything. What had happened between them in Istanbul hadn't been just a game, just a challenge to him—or had it? She still couldn't be sure from what he'd said...

'Listen, Zelda, if there was one thing I was certain of when we were together in Turkey it was that I didn't want my judgement about the take-over clouded by my very unprofessional feelings for you. But that was the only thing I *was* sure about... What I wasn't any good at sorting out was what was happening between us. You turned me on from the moment I met you, but because... well, of what had happened in the past... it seemed like a good idea to keep it on a physical level for a while—to give us both time. But it didn't work like that. You were too honest, and I couldn't admit then that what I felt for you was more than just sex. But, believe me, Magic Carpets was something totally separate. I'd known before I met you in Syria that you and Rick and Melanie were the kind of people I wanted to have working for me, and even the burglary didn't make any difference to that. I heard about it from Charles when I rang him from Istanbul after you'd left. We both decided he'd check out your insurance, and then go ahead with the offer.'

Zelda was in a turmoil—her body was reacting one way, her mind another, and her emotions, as always, caught somewhere in between.

'But I thought—he said you didn't contact him?' With every passing second he was confusing her more.

'I didn't—after that. I left it up to him because I went back to Eastern Turkey for a while, to finish some business I had to leave while I was driving a certain young lady to Istanbul.'

'You said you were going to Istanbul anyway!' she accused.

'True—I was. But not at that precise moment in time.'

'So that *was* all a ploy to get my carpet... I always knew you were a predator,' she said shakily. But she didn't mean anything she was saying. Unexpectedly, he had moved towards her. Half aware of his intention, she tried to side-step to avoid him, but he was too quick for her, slipping his arms round her waist to prevent her escape. The contact took all coherent thoughts from her head, as the pressure of his arms brought her up against him. She knew it was stupid to let him, but it was what she had been longing for.

His eyes were intensely green as they looked down into hers; she had forgotten how thick and dark his eyelashes were. It was just as well he was holding her—she wouldn't have been able to stand up on her own. Even her bones seemed to be melting—but it was crazy letting him do this to her. She had put her hands up feebly against his chest, but she had no will-power to push him away.

Then he said quickly, his voice unsteady, 'Zelda, I have to know—now—is there someone else?'

She stared at him blankly. Why? What was he...? 'Wh-what do you mean?'

'Since Istanbul—or is it the man you told me about?'

'Daniel? No, of course not! There isn't anyone——'

His arms tightened round her, and he was speaking more urgently. 'Then why didn't you want to come to the meeting? First you wouldn't talk to me on the phone, then you wouldn't enter into any of the negotiations, and you've been hostile ever since you appeared in my office this morning... What is it? Have you changed your mind about us? Is it only because of what I've done with the company or is it something else?'

She had never heard him like this, so impassioned, yet somehow unsure of himself. Bewildered, she stared up at him.

'You never rang—you never wrote—you never even tried to explain! I didn't know what to think... You were only going to be away two weeks, and you were going to ring me every day the second week and it was four weeks and you didn't ring at all!'

She couldn't go on even if she'd wanted to. He was holding her so tightly now she could hardly breathe, and she could feel his lips on her neck, and then on her ear, and the side of her face, in feverish little kisses that were all the more inexplicable because he was laughing.

But then when he ran his fingers up into her hair, pulling her head back so that she had to lift her face to him, and just as she thought he was going to kiss her properly—he didn't. Instead he looked down at her, the laughter still in his eyes.

'Have dinner with me tonight and I'll explain?'

'Why can't you tell me now?' she demanded, puzzled.

He gave her that familiar grin. 'Because I'm afraid you might refuse dinner, and I'm relying on your remarkable curiosity to provide an incentive...' She knew he was remembering that episode at Konya when her 'curiosity' had prompted her to unload his carpets on to a public square, but to her surprise he didn't tease her about it. Instead, the grin became an unexpectedly embarrassed one. 'Besides, I haven't got the courage to say everything I want to just yet...'

'What?'

But he clearly wasn't prepared to comment further.

Then, for what seemed like an age they stood there, looking at each other. None of it made sense to Zelda. She'd been telling herself she ought to hate him, just so something like this wouldn't happen. The real problem was still there—the question of their future as lovers—and yet here she was in his arms, virtually ready to let him do what he liked with her. But what exactly *was* he trying to do to her—prove to himself he still had the same power over her? Or prove it to her?

If that was his object, he didn't need to try. But it wasn't going to change the decisions she had already made: she wouldn't work for him—and, more important still, she wouldn't resume their affair. However much it might hurt to lose him now, it would be far worse if they continued without the commitment she needed. She wouldn't even attempt to discuss it now. The best thing would just be to go off quietly and find another job that would take her completely out of his life—she could even fly back to Turkey and set up something with Mehmet... only he'd probably be switching to work for Kalinsky's. But there was nothing to stop her branching out on her own...

That thought gave her the determination to try to push herself away from him.

For a second he was still, and then he released her. 'Come on. I'm taking you home,' he said quietly.

'But, Aram—the lunch! They'll be waiting for us——'

'No. I don't think they will. I'll pick you up at eight—that'll give you plenty of time to get ready for dinner.'

Her heart gave a little skip, and then she had to remind herself that, even if he did feel the same about her as he had in Istanbul, it still wouldn't be any good, because to go on with a casual affair with Aram would only destroy her in the end.

'I'd rather not go out to dinner. Thank you very much for asking me but...but I'm busy.'

'Cancel it—whatever it is,' he said curtly. 'I'm not giving you any choice.'

He pushed her unceremoniously outside, pulling the door to behind them and slipping the padlock once more through the hasp. 'Where exactly do you live? Putney, isn't it?'

But by the time they reached Parson's Green, where Dominic lived and where most of her things now were, she had been argued into telling him her brother's address, and into agreeing to go out with him, privately resolving that whatever the inducements after dinner she wouldn't go anywhere to be alone with him.

'I'll just wait on the doorstep no matter how long it takes,' he'd stated uncompromisingly. 'Even if it's breakfast, you'll have to give in eventually.'

Alone at Dominic's flat, it seemed as though she had hours to fill. Unwise though it might be, she knew she couldn't have resisted the temptation to spend a few hours with Aram. Just seeing him again, despite their differences, intensified all her old longing for him and she tried to delude herself that merely being in his company, talking to him, would be enough after the long weeks of absence. No, she told herself firmly, she wasn't going to restart their affair—but surely it wouldn't do any harm just to *eat* with him?

She supposed he had gone back to join the lunch party; she didn't mind that he hadn't given her any option about it—she would have chosen to go home in any case. Her imagination ran riot as she prowled about restlessly, unable to settle to anything, until finally she rang Melanie's home number.

'Who do you think I ought to apologise to for missing the lunch?' Her opening gambit was intended to elicit information about Aram, and whether or not he had rejoined the others.

'Pity you missed all the champagne!' Melanie sounded delightfully carefree. 'But I wouldn't bother about apologies. I think Charles had a pretty good idea what was going on between you and Aram. When neither of you had appeared by the time we got to the cheese, there were some quite imaginative speculations—probably accurate!'

'You mean Aram didn't appear at all?'

'No.' Melanie sounded quite surprised. 'We assumed he was with you. Actually, we all thought you'd gone to bed.'

'Melanie——!' But she didn't get a chance to continue.

'You mean you weren't with him?' Her friend was incredulous. 'Zelda, you must be mad to waste a man like that—he's *gorgeous*! You didn't have a row with him, did you?' she demanded. 'And whatever possessed you to call him a brigand? He's one of the nicest—and most generous—people I've met! You *do* realise he's leaving us completely free to do our own thing with Magic Carpets?'

There wasn't much point in going on with the call after that. If she wanted anyone to argue her out of her hopeless feelings for the subject of their conversation, it wasn't going to be Melanie.

CHAPTER TEN

THE ring at the doorbell later on that evening was so punctual there was little doubt as to who could be waiting outside Dominic's flat, and Zelda was determined to get out before her brother could inspect her escort. She had developed an acute sensitivity about the men in her life as far as her brothers were concerned, and she hadn't envisaged the possibility of a meeting when she'd decided to escape Aram by flying to Dominic's protection, and then confided to him tearfully, and at length, the history of their relationship.

She and Dominic arrived at the front door together, but her brother was a great deal larger than she was, and had no intention of giving ground.

'So you're the Franco-Armenian gun-runner, are you?' he greeted Aram tactlessly. 'Zelda's been boring me since yesterday with how you've bought her company and ruined her life. I'm very pleased that you're taking her out to dinner. I don't suppose you could make it breakfast as well——?'

'Dominic!'

'I was only going to add that you've drunk an entire quart of grapefruit juice since you arrived and there isn't any bread. If he can bring in the supplies of course he can have breakfast with us ... I don't suppose he'd take me out too, would he?'

Zelda ducked forward under her brother's arm, planting one high heel on his toe as she passed with the accuracy of long practice. She tried to pretend she wasn't disconcerted by the fraternal treachery. 'Aram, this is Dominic, my youngest brother. Dominic, this is Aram Kalinsky. Goodbye—Eeek!'

But Aram had had the same idea as herself about a quick getaway. Her hand firmly clasped in his, she was being pulled forwards almost on to his chest. 'Nice to meet you, Dominic,' he was saying. 'I gather you're in the same sort of busines as us—we must talk some time!' It amused her that his tone, although perfectly friendly, had the edge to it that could put a brother in his place, and the 'some time' sounded even vaguer than intended because by that time they were in the car, and any further exchanges were drowned by the roar of the engine.

Zelda didn't quite know what to think. It was difficult to sit beside him calmly, when she felt as though some of the champagne the others had had for lunch were fizzing in her blood. He was treating her all of a sudden as he had those last days in Istanbul, and that was dangerous in itself—despite all her resolutions about not resuming the relationship, she couldn't help wishing that he'd stop the car and kiss her the way he once had in Turkey, even though they would have caused an outrageous jam in the middle of all the London traffic.

It wasn't until they'd arrived outside an imposing town house in Kensington that it occurred to her he might not be taking her out to dinner in quite the way she had imagined.

'Where are we?' she demanded suspiciously, eyeing that aquiline profile with some apprehension.

'My house.'

'But I thought we were supposed to be going to a restaurant!'

'Did I say anything about a restaurant?' he queried innocently. 'I asked you to have dinner with me. That's not quite the same thing.'

They were standing under the pillared portico, which had an old-fashioned carriage lantern hanging from its ceiling. The front door looked wide enough to admit three abreast, but Aram had stood back to let her pass through first.

She eyed him warily. He was watching her with an expression it was hard to interpret. 'I—I never agreed to this!' she protested, irresolute.

She'd counted on the fact that they would be surrounded by waiters and other couples out for the evening to keep her to her decision; dinner alone in his house was an entirely different matter. Her immediate impulse was to dart out into the street after a passing taxi and put as much distance between herself and Aram as she could. But, before she was able to take one hasty step in the direction of the pavement, she found herself being propelled firmly forward into the house, her body, as always, betraying her into the very thing she thought she'd decided against.

The hall was magnificent—not just on account of its size, but because the collection of mirrors, rugs and fine pieces of furniture gave an impression of elegance and wealth beyond anything she had seen before outside some stately home. Her earlier reluctance to enter the house turned swiftly into astonishment.

'You *live* here?'

The incredulity in her tone wasn't lost on him, and he laughed. 'It's the family home—technically mine now. The result of my grandfather's ill-gotten gains of course—gun-running, drug pushing and the like.'

She saw the glint in his eyes and looked away. He had an effective line in making her feel foolish. In the romantic setting of the Syrian desert it was easy to let your imagination run away with you, and a tall hawk-nosed stranger could become a predatory brigand in no time at all. Now, in the context of the considerable family wealth she'd somehow never connected with him, she remembered the other image that had come into her mind—a Roman emperor off an old coin. Suddenly, that was the image that seemed to fit him much better, and it endowed him with a remoteness that suited these rather awe-inspiring surroundings. She felt newly nervous of him, and aware of him in a way she'd never been before, as though he were a stranger to her yet again.

Then he was standing behind her, helping her off with her coat, and the sense of his nearness as his fingers brushed her naked shoulders made her spine prickle—and that was another thing. She had dressed to go out to a glamorous restaurant, not to spend the evening in the intimate surroundings of a private house.

There was a pause. He was holding her coat, but she still had one hand caught in the sleeve, and she could feel his eyes on her.

She stepped forward to free herself, moving away from him quickly. 'I wasn't expecting to spend the evening quite like this,' she said awkwardly, trying to turn it into a joke. 'Perhaps I should have worn jeans or something.' She wished her voice didn't betray her nervousness quite so obviously.

'You look wonderful,' he said quietly. 'And I was appreciating a rather beautiful bare back I haven't seen for far too long. Come into the drawing-room and have a drink.' She was glad he didn't seem to expect any response to the personal remark he had just made, and she tried not to let herself be affected by the warmth she heard in his voice.

She agreed to the first drink he suggested to her, incapable of making a decision, and then perched uncomfortably on one of the elegant Regency sofas. The drawing-room was high-ceilinged, with chandeliers and mirrors and gilt-framed paintings, and the thought of Aram as its owner seemed to have dried up any ideas she might have for conversation.

Her throat felt tight with nerves. She gave a half-husky, half-squeaky little cough. 'Do you have a cook?' she asked foolishly.

Aram was standing by a long antique sideboard looking at her across the width of the room, a decanter in his hands. His mouth gave a familiar quirk. 'What's the matter—isn't my cooking good enough for you?'

'I didn't mean—I just didn't think...' She would never have imagined he could have made her feel so awkward in his company.

'We've got a faithful friend and retainer, who's worked for the family since my grandfather's day. She's a housekeeper-cum-cook for special occasions, but Helen offered to make the supper for tonight.'

'Your sister? Is she here?' She didn't know whether to feel relieved or apprehensive. Another rich and successful Kalinsky might prove too much for her—on the other hand, his sister's presence might restrain him if he'd any plans for seduction.

'No—she's in *Giselle* at Covent Garden tonight, dancing in the *corps de ballet*. She was very sorry she couldn't meet you.' He was halfway across the room with a glass in each hand. 'You'll see her in the morning.'

What?

She shot off the sofa as though it had suddenly become a bed of live coals.

'What's that supposed to mean?' she demanded, her voice splitting into a panicky squeak. 'You've got me here under false pretences and you know it! There's no way I'm spending the night here with you and if you think you can just carry on where we left off in Istanbul, Aram Kalinsky, you'd better think again!'

He stopped, and she wasn't sure how to read the keen look he gave her from those blue-green eyes. Deliberately, he turned towards the marble fireplace, setting the glasses down on the mantelpiece, and as he did so she edged further along the sofa in the direction of the door. If it came to fight or flight, she had no doubts now about which she'd choose.

But, again, it was one of those disconcerting moments when she felt as though he could read her mind. Instead of approaching her as she had expected, he crossed straight to the door, shut it firmly, and then leaned against it, arms folded. Several yards of floor between them, they faced each other.

'The reason I brought you here tonight was because I know you of old, Zelda—I haven't forgotten other restaurants where we've sat across a table completely incapable of communicating with each other because you've got up on your high horse about something you won't explain, and you've used the fact we're in a public place to keep me at a distance.'

'*I've* got up on my high horse——!'

'Perhaps you'd like to tell me how you see it, then?'

She bit her lip, and glared at him. Typical! He was working everything to his advantage as usual—and he wasn't going to give her a chance to gather her wits.

'Shall I tell you how I see it? That is, if I can be sure of "seeing" any of it,' he added bitterly. 'You fought me off at first because you said you didn't want just casual sex—it had to mean something. When we finally made it, I thought it was something quite special for both of us—but we both needed time to think about what was happening between us. Then, by the time you left Istanbul, you told me you couldn't wait until I got back to England too—you even wanted me to phone you when I told you I'd be out in the wilds of Eastern Turkey miles from anywhere! And if that all doesn't add up to some sort of commitment on your side, I don't know what does.

'Then I finally get back, after four of the most frustrating weeks of my life, and what happens? You don't want to know me. You won't speak to me on the phone, you won't see me, you won't even come to a meeting with four other people present—a meeting which in the long run was entirely to your advantage. So I'm forced to the conclusion that you've met someone else, but, when I ask you, you assure me you haven't. I save your company, give you *carte blanche* to go on doing your job just the way you want—and your brother tells me you think I've ruined your life. Would you care to explain—or shall I just cut to what I really want to say?'

She was used to the final note of sarcasm—she had seen Aram so angry before that she had been genuinely frightened, and she had even known him to be hurt by her reactions—but she had never known him quite like this. She couldn't define that mixture of anger and control and whatever else it was in that rough, edgy voice, and she was at a loss as to how to react.

He was still leaning against the door, hands thrust into trouser pockets. A familiar lock of crisp, blue-black hair hung untidily over his forehead, and the green eyes were enigmatic as always.

They stared at each other, tension pulled tight as a wire between them.

'You accuse me of not communicating!' she blurted out at last, unable to bear the strained silence any longer. 'But what about *you*? You won't tell me anything! First you go on letting me think you're some dangerous sort of crook, then when I try to find out some answers for myself you behave as though I'd *stolen* all your carpets instead of just had a harmless look at them!'

'You can't blame me for your own over-active imagination.'

He sounded curt and dismissive—just as he did at his most cold and sarcastic, the way she most disliked him. He could switch so quickly: almost loving one minute, and hatefully remote the next.

'Oh, so I suppose it was my fault when you wouldn't tell me you were a carpet dealer when I first asked you!' she said bitterly. 'And what about the other questions you wouldn't answer? Like how you really felt about me, or why exactly you found it so difficult to phone me from Turkey when you had four whole weeks to make the call?' Now she'd started she might as well say it all and then after tonight it would be stupid to go on seeing him. So she would make a definite end: just let all the misery of uncertainty and resentment of the past few weeks well up in her now unchecked.

'You seem to think you've got a right to make all sorts of decisions about my life! Everything from interfering with my Syrian deal to taking over my business! And even this morning—you never *asked* me if I wanted to go back to lunch with the others, you just *told* me I was going to have dinner with you and then disposed of me like a—a consignment of not very valuable old mats you'd just bought!'

She knew she was being unreasonable, and was angry with herself—and him—for making her feel like this. But it didn't matter any longer what she said to him. The sooner he was out of her life the better—they didn't seem to be able to meet for five minutes without fighting.

'*And* you expect me to be able to read your mind!' she went on furiously. 'You knew how I felt about you—I told you that night in the hotel on the way to Istanbul—and if you think things have changed then it's your fault and I've already told you why...' She knew she was getting herself so worked up she would start to cry, but the intensity of her own emotional reaction was taking even her by surprise. 'And don't tell me I already knew you were crazy about me! It's no good just being "crazy about" someone—it only means you want them in bed and I'm not going on with an affair with you, Aram——' She saw him open his mouth to say something, but she hadn't finished yet. 'You're impossible! You never tell me *anything* I need to hear—and you...you haven't even said where you spent the afternoon!'

'Zelda——' In a couple of strides he was across the room, but she knew what he was going to do and darted away from him, round the back of the sofa.

'Don't touch me!'

'Just shut up and listen for a minute——'

'And don't you dare tell me to shut up ever again!' And then she began to cry in earnest.

There was no way she could escape into the hall, but as she turned through a blur of tears she saw panelled double doors that must lead into another room and ran towards them.

He reached her as she stumbled through them. When she felt his arms round her she told herself she should resist, but instead of pushing him away she found herself clinging to him and sobbing helplessly. His hand slid up into her hair, and he was caressing her as he held her against him.

'Zelda...don't cry. I didn't mean it to be like this...' Then he was murmuring only half-articulate endearments until the sobs subsided a little. 'Sweetheart, please stop. I'd much rather have you quarrelling with me than crying—I can't bear to think I've done this to you...'

In spite of everything, it felt wonderful to be in his arms again, and she indulged in the tears far longer than she needed purely for the luxury of having him comfort her. The sensation of that strong, reassuring body so close to her own was something she'd missed for too long.

Eventually, she gave a sniff, and wiped her eyes with the back of her hand. 'Well, if it's only guilt that's making you so nice to me...' she said unevenly. And then, 'I haven't got a handkerchief.'

He pulled a clean square of white linen from his pocket, and she was vaguely aware that some small hard object fell on the floor as he did so. She took the handkerchief from him, and blew her nose, while he bent down to pick up whatever it was that had fallen.

'What's that?' she asked curiously, her voice still unsteady. When he stood up it was hidden in his hand, and he didn't answer her directly. Suddenly he looked almost awkward, as though he wasn't sure what he was going to say.

'If you wanted to know what I was doing this afternoon you only had to ask me.'

'What *were* you doing?'

'Trying to find this.' Abruptly, he held it out on his palm.

The ring was set with a single large sapphire, circled by diamonds. It winked blue fire at her, reflecting the light of the chandeliers in the next room.

'It was my grandmother's...but I wasn't sure where we kept it. I only discovered it was locked in a bank vault when it was almost too late to get it out... You seem to like blue rings.'

She stared down at it, and then at her own slim ringless fingers. Those turquoises had all been part of her tourist act. But what Aram was offering was far too valuable to accept as a casual gift. It looked like an engagement ring. Her heart began to beat more erratically, but she didn't dare let herself hope. Why couldn't he *say* what he meant? He had sounded so hesitant, but she was learning more about her handsome carpet dealer in a few minutes than she had known all the time she was with him in Turkey.

His flashes of temper, and equally of humour, and his early and honest acknowledgement of the physical magnetism between them, had led her to assume that he could be open about his emotions when he wanted to be. But she was realising now that he found it hard to put his deepest feelings into words, or perhaps even to admit them to himself.

She remembered how, that night on the road to Istanbul, he had given only the briefest sketch of his relationship with Gina, but from the outline she had guessed that he had found it far more traumatic than he was prepared to admit. She now realised that, even though he seemed to have passed all the barriers erected by that earlier relationship, he still found it hard to ask her to marry him. And now he was so uncertain of her response he was actually afraid she might say no! It was almost incredible to her when all along she had assumed her own feelings must be obvious to him. He had seemed to be able to read her mind so often.

'What is it?' she asked again, suddenly breathless with a new and giddy happiness, but determined to make him spell it out.

He was looking down at her, enigmatic as ever, those extraordinary blue-green eyes full of some emotion she could only guess at. She slipped her arms round his neck, pressing close to him, and began to kiss the side of his chin. 'Aram,' she said in her most long-suffering tones in between kisses, 'aren't you *ever* going to ask me?'

But she knew what his response would be and clasped him even tighter as his arms went round her, and his mouth claimed hers with an impatience that literally took her breath away. When finally he broke off the kiss, he buried his face in her hair and she could feel his heart beating thunderously against hers and his breathing as uneven as her own.

'Marry me,' he said, so low she wasn't sure even now she had heard the words rightly.

At last...

'You're really *not* very good at talking about your feelings, are you?' she teased softly.

'You were so hostile this morning, I thought you were going to refuse,' he confessed gruffly, his face still in her hair. So he had finally answered one of her questions—he was, in the end, admitting that he loved her. But he had kept her waiting long enough, and two could play at that game...

There was more she wanted to know before she would give him his answer. It would no longer make any difference what he said, but she wanted him to satisfy her curiosity. 'And that phone call from Turkey that didn't happen?' she prompted, knowing that if she didn't get her answer soon, it would be a long time before either of them was interested again in the kind of communication between them now. He was holding her too close against him for her to be unaware of the effect she was having on him.

He looked down at her, and mingled with a sort of wry amusement was some of that earlier awkwardness.

'I don't think you're going to believe this. But it all started when I ran over somebody's goat.'

Her eyes began to sparkle gleefully. 'I believe you, Aram,' she said sweetly. 'In fact it sounds quite predictable. You were driving too fast...'

And that was another thing he wasn't very good at— admitting he was wrong!

There was a familiar quirk to the side of his mouth, and, unexpectedly, he admitted, 'Yes... well. All right,

I was. But to cut a long story short, it was a Kurdish goat.'

Silence.

'And that's the story?' she demanded incredulously.

'More or less. Yes.'

'Definitely *less*! You really don't waste words do you?' She began to laugh. 'What am I going to do with you? So I'm supposed to guess what happened from that?'

From the glint of humour in those enigmatic eyes she knew he was teasing her. 'I thought that over-active imagination of yours could supply the rest...' Then he relented. 'All right, I was close to the Iranian border, which, you'll be surprised to hear, isn't a neat little line drawn across a lot of wild mountains——'

'Aram——!' she said warningly.

'I'd been after some carpets a contact of mine had told me about, and by the time one thing had led to another I was in a Kurdish area and I'd run over the damned goat, and very nearly run over an armed Kurd who leapt out of nowhere to demand compensation.'

'You could have been shot!' Suddenly she was horrified by the possibilities of what he was telling her. The Kurds living along the Turkish borders were a law unto themselves.

'Well, yes. I suppose I could. Except that it occurred to him that I'd be more valuable alive than dead, and after that we got on rather well, and I ended up under a sort of house arrest in a mountain village. They were very hospitable, but couldn't decide what to do with me.'

'Why didn't you just pay the man for his goat, or offer to get him two in compensation? That's what I'd have done!'

His expression changed, and he grinned down at her. 'All right, little Miss Smarty Pants, so next time I'll take you with me—which is what I would have done anyway if you hadn't been so keen to get back to London. And now tell me how you'd have got us out of it with only the equivalent of about one pound sterling in Turkish lira?'

'But I thought you said you were buying carpets?'

'I had been. And it had turned out to be a more expensive expedition than I'd expected. The rest of my money was safely stowed away with my passport and all my papers back in the town where I was staying.'

She fought the temptation to point out that she wouldn't have got into that situation in the first place, and then reflected that, in carpet buying, you never knew what might happen. You might even find yourself stranded in the desert with a broken-down car and a stranger, or sleeping in a cave somewhere . . . 'OK, I give in. So how did you do it?'

'Luck,' he admitted with a rueful grin. 'By the time I'd parted with what money I'd got, and my gold watch, and most of the tools out of the car, and a valuable carpet they could resell at a profit——'

'Not *my* carpet?' she demanded quickly.

'Pity, I didn't think of that.' He drew a teasing line down her cheek with one finger. 'No, I didn't have it with me . . . Anyway, by the time I'd paid it all out in bribes, or compensation or whatever, and they decided they didn't want to use me as a hostage to gain some political advantage, and quite a lot of time had passed, someone turned up by chance who knew a dealer I knew. He turned out to be a cousin of an influential villager and persuaded them to let me go. I'd have got home a couple of days sooner flying from Ankara, but all your carpets were in Istanbul and I'd promised you I'd bring them back safely. I drove virtually non-stop across Turkey and got straight on to a plane from Istanbul— carpets and all. Now are you satisfied?'

She shook her head solemnly. 'A really resourceful person would have sent a note by carrier pigeon.'

His arms tightened round her. 'Oh, and what should I have said? "Held prisoner by hostile Kurds—rescue me"?'

'No,' she said consideringly, looking at him sideways. '"I love you" would have done just as well.'

He began to laugh. 'And would telling you I loved you now make up for such a glaring omission? Zelda, I can't bear the suspense any longer—are you going to marry me or not?'

'Proposals are supposed to be romantic!' she protested. 'Yours wasn't. You made me cry.'

'OK, so I'm not very good at the romantic bits.'

'You were all right in Turkey.'

He smiled down at her. 'Turkey has some natural advantages which are lacked by my office—which was the first place I'd planned to propose to you, only you were in such a bad mood there was no chance of getting anywhere near the topic—and your garage—sorry, *warehouse*—which was the second location I had in mind. But what could be more romantic than where I'm proposing to you now?'

'What do you mean?' she demanded, puzzled.

'Zelda, do you mean to tell me that after making all that fuss about it, you don't even recognise your own Magic Carpet when you're standing on it?'

'My...my carpet?' She hadn't even looked at it.

'*My* carpet,' he said firmly. 'Unless you marry me.'

She slipped her hands up into his hair, pulling his head down to her. 'How could you ever have imagined I'd refuse?' she whispered.

Everything happened very quickly after that. She wasn't sure quite how the ring found itself on her finger, or how it was that in the middle of an embrace which, she was half aware, should have ended up in one of the many bedrooms the house surely possessed, she found herself on the floor with Aram lying on top of her. He was looking down at her in the subdued light that fell through the open doors to the drawing-room. The weight of that tall, powerful body on hers was wonderfully familiar, and she could hardly bear it when he broke off what he was doing.

'Four weeks has been like a lifetime,' he said unsteadily. 'I knew how much I loved you the minute your plane took off from Istanbul—I'd have done anything to get you back with me then. I don't know why I wouldn't admit it before, except that at first I was so determined not to get seriously involved again. I'm not even sure now what I assumed would happen—some sort of casual affair, I suppose—but the effect you had on me was far too powerful for that. You surprised me in too many ways... I've wanted you so much. I don't think I can wait any longer...'

The way he was caressing her left her in no doubt of his desire, and she had only just enough presence of mind left to object, 'Aram—we can't—not here. Supposing your sister comes in?'

He began to kiss her ear, and then the side of her neck. 'There's no one else in the house and Helen won't be back for hours...'

As always, their effect on each other was like sparks of fire, quickly flickering up into a mutual flame that would soon consume them both. The touch of his hands was driving her senseless—she was already practically naked. Then suddenly there was that endearing quirk of humour at the side of his mouth despite the urgency she could sense in his body. 'You know what Magic Carpets are supposed to do, don't you?' he asked.

She moved restlessly under him. 'Yes...yes—don't stop now, Aram, please...'

'If it doesn't, I'm going to prosecute you under the Trade Descriptions Act...'

She had no success in feigning annoyance. 'Aram, this is meant to be *romantic*!' The mock reproof was a little too breathless to be convincing. Then she added, 'It'll serve you right for taking over an entire company to get one rug!'

Her aggrieved tones provoked the familiar low laugh. 'One rug—and one woman. Just as I told you I would... Now shut your eyes and pretend this is real romance... We're in some filthy old cave full of draughts and rats where you've just said you'll marry me and we can spend the rest of our lives together—flying carpets every time we need to take a break from quarrelling...'

So he had made good that threat, or boast, or promise, or whatever it had been, and he sounded infuriatingly pleased with himself. But in the end they had *both* got what they wanted—something so much simpler than all those games and bargains they'd been playing at. Each other.

'Aram,' she protested weakly, 'after all the times I wanted you to talk to me and you wouldn't, why does it have to be *now* that you suddenly find so much to say?'

'Zelda,' he said, but only after a very, very long time. 'You know, I think you probably *could* have got this carpet from your Syrian cheaper than I did . . .'

Now he tells me!

But it wasn't something she was going to argue about. For a while, anyway.

my VALENTINE 1992

Celebrate the most romantic day of the year with
MY VALENTINE 1992—a sexy new collection of four
romantic stories written by our famous Temptation
authors:

GINA WILKINS
KRISTINE ROLOFSON
JOANN ROSS
VICKI LEWIS THOMPSON

My Valentine 1992—an exquisite escape into a romantic
and sensuous world.

 Harlequin Books

VAL-92-R

HARLEQUIN
PROUDLY PRESENTS
A DAZZLING NEW CONCEPT IN ROMANCE FICTION

One small town—twelve terrific love stories

Welcome to Tyler, Wisconsin—a town full of people
you'll enjoy getting to know, memorable friends and
unforgettable lovers, and a long-buried secret that
lurks beneath its serene surface....

JOIN US FOR A YEAR IN THE LIFE OF TYLER

Each book set in Tyler is a self-contained love story;
together, the twelve novels stitch the fabric of a
community.

LOSE YOUR HEART TO TYLER!

The excitement begins in March 1992, with
WHIRLWIND, by Nancy Martin. When lively, brash
Liza Baron arrives home unexpectedly, she moves
into the old family lodge, where the silent and
mysterious Cliff Forrester has been living in seclusion
for years....

WATCH FOR ALL TWELVE BOOKS
OF THE TYLER SERIES
Available wherever Harlequin books are sold

Janet Dailey
Americana

A romantic tour of America through fifty favorite
Harlequin Presents novels, each one set in a different
state, and researched by Janet and her husband, Bill.
A journey of a lifetime in one cherished collection.

Don't miss the romantic stories set in these states:

Available wherever
Harlequin books are sold.

JD-MAR